Dear Pat,

You may not like it, nor may you find the time to read it, but at least you'll have a copy signed by the author

With love

Roy

R Bond

A ONE-OFF

My Name is Bond –
Roy Bond

MINERVA PRESS
LONDON
ATLANTA MONTREUX SYDNEY

A ONE-OFF

ISBN 0 75410 159 2

First Published 1998 by
MINERVA PRESS
195 Knightsbridge
London SW7 1RE

Printed in Great Britain for Minerva Press

A ONE-OFF

To all my family and friends

About the Author

Roy Bond was born in Hampstead, London, in 1931. He retired as an inspector with the Metropolitan Police after thirty years' service. He was then an office services manager for fourteen years with a financial factoring company based in Croydon. He resides in Harrow, Middlesex and is married with four children and nine grandchildren.

The first and probably only 'one-off' novel by the author, in which his characters commit their only 'one-off' crime of Incest, Murder, Theft, Rape and TDA, (Taking and Driving Away a motor vehicle without the consent of the owner thereof).

Chapter One

Martyn Burgess had lain there in the total darkness listening to the dull ominous drone up above and he offered up a silent prayer. He wasn't religious, he was only eight years old; but he had been sent to Sunday school fairly regularly and believed that it was right and proper to pray to God in such circumstances. In any case it did afford him some comfort to talk to some Being, and took his mind off the sickening fear that started to well up inside him most nights. His weekly sojourn to the local church hall, along with his friends was no doubt not entirely for his religious education but more than likely to give his parents and the parents of his friends, time to themselves on a Sunday afternoon. But all that had ceased some time ago. It was only a few months since his last birthday when his mother had come to visit him in the then modern three up, two down semi, with –joy of joys – a garden, in suburbia where he had been hastily evacuated in the forlorn hope of safety.

It was inconceivable that the authorities could have thought that it would be safer to be a mere fifteen miles further out of London, although in fairness to them it was no doubt due to the last minute panic of parents such as Martyn's, who made the sudden decision to have their offspring evacuated.

Ironically, Rickmansworth in Hertfordshire, did sustain some bomb damage. As far as Martyn was concerned, however, he was as much in the countryside as Richmal Crompton's famous William. Martyn, like William and his gang, could now ramble in the chalk pits, gambol over the fields, pick blackberries in the hedgerows, and he could play in the rear garden. There he got his first taste of the sweet aroma of burning garden waste and bracken in the garden bonfires.

Although times were relatively hard, his mother had given him for his eighth birthday a present of an annual-sized book about a family of rabbits: not *Watership Down* type of rabbits but *Rupert Bear* type of rabbits dressed in human clothes.

He loved that book. Spaced throughout the book had been six or so extra thick pages, which had each contained a highly coloured picture of the characters as depicted in the story, the whole of each picture being cut out as a jigsaw puzzle. Each one was held in place by a thin transparent film of cellophane. Feeling very happy at that particular time Martyn had declined his mother's offer to take him home. He had been away from her for only six weeks or so but to her it was an eternity; she missed him dearly but felt it was her motherly duty to leave him in assumed safety. His sister though, some six and a half years his senior, had already returned to the fold, all believing that she was not really a child and should be out in the world earning her living.

Come the actual time of his mother's departure a wave of loneliness welled up within him and he tearfully requested to accompany her and return home. His mother had joyfully packed his clothes into his suitcase and bid a thankful farewell to his wartime foster parents.

It wasn't a long journey by the old Metropolitan Line train, in the single compartments with the heavy swinging hinged doors (slam doors as they are now referred to) to their mews flat in Canfield Place at Finchley Road in Hampstead, north-west London. On their arrival they were greeted as they entered the living room by Martyn's father and his sister. Martyn was also greeted by the family pet dog, a black, white and a patch of tan wire-haired terrier mongrel.

'Hello Bobby!' said Martyn, rubbing the dog's ears.

His family laughed, because in his few weeks away with his foster family he had been taught to sound his H's and to speak with an upper middle-class accent and they were expecting him to say ''Allo Bob' in a more typically London accent.

It is astonishing what a child can learn in just a few short weeks. The man of the house where Martyn had been billeted would always insist, at teatime, that Martyn put down his sandwich or cake back on the plate after each mouthful and not sit there holding it in his hand. Martyn's mother had been highly impressed with his table manners but did little to see that they persisted.

During the blitz the family had come home one morning from the basement air raid shelter under a nearby department store to find that Bobby, in terror of the bangs of the bombs and gunfire, had practically gnawed his way through the living room door in a frantic attempt to escape. It was then that Martyn's father decided that it would be most humane to have their faithful friend put down; not only because the dog could continue to be stressed by bombs and gunfire but also because of the progressing difficulty of obtaining food for the animal in times of rationing. There were tearful farewells when Bobby was taken off to suffer the fate of many of his kind in those early days of the war.

So now Martyn lay there in bed at night alone, or so he felt; his parents and sister were only a room away. Frightened, he prayed that the aeroplane droning up above, (not with the modern present-day jet engine, but the heavy throbbing engine driving the propellers, or to be exact the airscrews of the engines in those times) were not being flown by the German crews of the Luftwaffe, equipped with bombs to rain down on him and London. He prayed that they were our own bombers on their way to do just such an acceptable thing to the enemy. But his prayers remained unanswered.

Canfield Place, London, NW3 was a cobbled cul-de-sac mews situated between the London Transport Metropolitan and Bakerloo lines (the latter now renamed the Jubilee line) on the north side and the non-electrified line for the steam trains, where they disappeared into the mouth of the tunnel allowing them access to London and Marylebone station.

One night these railway lines running parallel must have presented an ideal target for the German bomb aimer flying high above. He released his stick of six bombs and was unfortunate in that only his last bomb actually scored a direct hit on the non-electrified line, some twenty yards or so before it disappeared into the bowels of Hampstead under the shops. The bomb also destroyed a row of single storey private garages in Canfield Place. The five previous bombs of the stick demolished the large Victorian houses whose rear gardens backed onto the railway line in question on the north side of Broadhurst Gardens, which ran between Finchley Road and West Hampstead. Little did young Martyn realise it then that in spite of moving away from the area at the age of ten, he was, many years later, to have an unsavoury association with West Hampstead once more.

The only other prayer uttered by Martyn at that age had been, 'Please God, don't let Mummy and Daddy fight any more.'

It was unlikely that his parents fought any more than many other married couples, although they may have been more violent towards each other than most. His father believed that his wife's behaviour was influenced by the phases of the moon and she would turn on him every full moon.

In those unenlightened days there was no open talk or general knowledge and understanding of PMT by most males, with their Victorian attitudes of the previous generations. This obviously influenced his parents' relationship with each other as they continued to have their periodic fights and they were physical fights, not just arguments.

The fact that neither of his prayers had been answered had the affect of teaching Martyn at an early age that one didn't get what one wanted, fervently or otherwise, just by asking for it, especially from God. In spite of this it was many years before he ceased the nightly ritual of saying his prayers.

⋆

Indeed many years had now since passed by. Mentally and even physically he had not felt any detrimental affect of those passing years. He still thought and felt like a young man. The blow would come whenever he saw his reflection in the mirror or shop window. It would take a while to recognise the grey-haired old bugger as himself. It was far worse when he compared recent photographs with the old; but that is life for all of us as time passes at the same speed for everyone.

Nevertheless he was still regarded as looking young for his age and people were often surprised and possibly envious to learn that he had retired.

He was now on his own after a failed marriage and another failed association of cohabitation. He didn't regard himself as hard to get on with but realised that there must be faults on both sides of all failed associations. So he was free, not financially, though, as he still provided for his wife and home where he had his own bedroom and maintained the house and gardens. It was a financially convenient arrangement more beneficial than selling the property and dividing the proceeds.

So he was free to go wherever he pleased, which was how he came to be driving on his own with a packed suitcase in the boot of his five-year-old Toyota saloon. Being on his own he didn't really need a family saloon but old habits die hard, although he occasionally toyed with the idea of getting a two-seater sports job. But there again, he didn't consider the extra insurance premiums that would be required for a sports car justification for any such change, and he could get from A to B just as easily and comfortably with his present car.

He was driving through Acton behind a red Toyota MR2. The traffic wardens must have been working very diligently in this part of London because the kerbside was completely clear of parked vehicles, allowing for the two lanes of traffic the road was marked with white lines for. At least, two lanes of traffic would have been possible but for a rust bucket of a brown Nissan saloon which was in front of the MR2 and hogging the centre of the road, straddling the centre white line of the westbound side of road. The driver of the MR2 sounded the horn a number of times as she tried to overtake. Every time she tried to do so, so the brake lights of the Nissan came on and it stayed firmly in the middle of the two lanes.

Martyn felt sympathy for the driver when at last the MR2 sounded its horn and pulled out to the right and commenced to overtake. As it did so the Nissan swerved to the right forcing the MR2 into the path of the oncoming traffic. It managed to get safely by, but only just, as it cut back to the left seconds before possible impact with a sturdy petrol tanker. The MR2 screeched to a halt, forcing the Nissan and the following traffic to likewise stop. The driver of the MR2 got out.

She was young, slim, wearing a black sweater and tight figure-hugging black corduroy slacks with fairly high-heeled shoes. Looking at her, Martyn wondered how she could manage to drive in such shoes. He also expected her to give the driver of the Nissan a piece of her mind. Instead she turned away and sauntered, with her hips swinging provocatively, towards the front of her car and opened the bonnet.

Martyn then realised that the MR2 was a rear engined car, and he gazed open-mouthed as she took out a pickaxe handle and, walking just as slowly to the front of the Nissan, calmly smashed both headlamps. She hesitated momentarily but the Nissan driver remained behind the steering wheel. The young woman retraced her steps just as slowly, replaced the pickaxe handle, and before getting back into her car she gave the Nissan driver the V-sign. Although she hadn't hurried in her actions the whole incident was over in a matter of minutes. She drove away quickly and the Nissan then roared off in hot pursuit.

Martyn and the following traffic followed at a more normal pace. At the next set of traffic lights Martyn stopped at the red light in the offside lane along side the Nissan. The Nissan was once more in front of the MR2. There was a young Asian male leaning on the bonnet of the MR2 shouting some obscenity at the young woman. Martyn actually had his hand on his door handle, about to go to the assistance of the young woman when he stopped himself. It was all very well being public-spirited but other people's business didn't justify any violence, coupled with the possibility of getting a knife in the ribs. The vehicle behind sounded its horn and Martyn noticed that the lights had changed to green. He was supposed to be setting out to enjoy himself, not get involved in the aggravations of road rage. He put the clutch in, engaged first gear and drove off, as did all the other traffic in the offside lane behind him.

Like Martyn the other drivers were well aware of the implications of road rage. Martyn turned up the volume of his radio which was tuned to 105.4 Melody Radio. It was pleasant soothing music just right to soothe the temper of frustrated modern motorists, even if the younger generation referred to it as 'supermarket music'.

It was early in the year as he drove, with the sun low in a sky which was practically devoid of clouds. Therefore the sun shone directly into his eyes, making the task more hazardous whenever he was driving in that direction. These hazardous conditions were also exacerbated if rain had recently fallen making the road surface into a mirror, reflecting the sun up into his eyes. He disliked driving on motorways, finding it excruciatingly boring, especially if he was not in a hurry to get anywhere in particular – which he wasn't. He was pleased therefore to veer off left from the motorway, endeavouring to adjust quickly to a more slower speed. He was soon happy to be traversing much more pleasant roads with pleasurable scenery. Having passed from a Motorway to A Class roads, he was now moving sedately along a B Class road. His was the only vehicle on the road, which was very surprising in this modern age of the internal combustion engine. It reminded him of years past when he had last driven in Eire when you could have driven for miles and only be met by a horse and cart or lone cyclist.

Now he occasionally came across evidence of tractors crossing from one field to another where they had deposited mud on the road. He eventually came to a small crossroad and although he came to a standstill at the junction, he only needed to slow down as he could clearly see the other road was equally devoid of traffic.

Just after crossing the junction he was most surprised to be confronted with a lone female hitch-hiker. As he approached, she turned towards him and raised her left arm in the air with her thumb extended skywards motioning towards the way he was going. He was surprised on two counts. One, that even in this day and age of numerous reports in the media of rape and murder of lone females, some even in their own homes, let alone in fairly remote spots such as this, she had not heeded the sensational reporting of such cases. Two, that she should have chosen such a quiet road to hitch a lift. She would have a far better chance of a lift on a much busier road.

Martyn was well aware that such a tempting offer (offer of what?) could well be a decoy to enable her six feet tall athletic boyfriend, hiding close by, to pounce on an unsuspecting gallant knight of the road and mug him of his valuables and even of the car itself. He therefore drove past her for a few feet before stopping in order to make the girl come to him, thus ensuring that she was indeed on her own.

As he sat looking in his rear-view mirror watching her approach, he pondered on the media's and consequently the public's use of the word 'mugging'. Why on earth did they have to change from the perfectly good old fashioned word of 'robbery'? Who would ever dream of calling Dick Turpin a Highway Mugger? It was, he mused, another infuriating piece of slang imported from the U S of A. There, having a set pattern of offenders regularly committing crimes in a small area, they had on police files photographs of convicted offenders which victims were invited to peruse in the hope of identifying the perpetrator of the crime committed against them. As these photographs were of the face or 'mug' they became known as 'mugshots' and consequently the offenders became known as 'muggers'. The crime of robbery henceforth became known as mugging and was now so described in all dictionaries. All this flashed through his mind in the fraction of time it took for her to reach his car.

As she approached, he wound down the front passenger door window. Well, he didn't have to lean over and physically wind it down, all he had to do was press the appropriate button for the electrically operated window to glide effortlessly down. He now looked at the pleasant smiling face now framed in the window as she leaned down to look in. He could see that she was more a young woman than a girl, which subconsciously suited him better. She was not unattractive, having even white teeth and curly fair to light-brown hair. For some reason it appeared to him as being too neat. He expected hitch-hikers to have lank damp hair cut short in a pageboy style or held back in a pony-tail and therefore far easier to manage for such a mode of travel.

Something didn't seem quite right, but it went quickly from his thoughts as she said, 'Hi, can you give me a lift?'

Chapter Two

Sally Wainwright had lain there in the darkness listening to the ominous creak of wood against wood as the heavy and unsteady footfalls crept agonisingly slowly up the stairs. She was then also only eight years of age but she was fully aware of what was about to happen. As she lay in the darkness she too offered up a silent prayer. She wasn't religious, she didn't know the existence of the word let alone the meaning of it and she had never been to Sunday school. Nevertheless she knew well enough that what was about to happen yet again was wrong and evil.

She heard his sonorous breathing. Very soon she would feel the weight upon her bed and smell the stench of alcohol on his breath as he nuzzled his unshaven face into the warmth of her smooth and tender young neck. She stiffened involuntarily, her little body rigid as a board, but it would afford her no protection whatsoever. He had already pulled his pants and trousers down to his ankles. He took her hand and placed it on his stiff penis while his other hand slid slowly up between her thin white thighs. Then his rough fingers probed deeper and deeper into her while he guided her hand faster and faster until he nearly climaxed and then forced himself into her, replacing his fingers with his penis until he ejaculated and lay heavily on top of her regaining his breath.

Sally's prayers were never answered; his visits were regular, always culminating in the very act of incest as it had years earlier with her older sisters Maisey and Josie. She hated her father. Neither did she like her mother very much. She felt sorry for her, certainly, but she was sure that her mother was fully aware of what was going on and very much resented the fact that she did nothing to come to the aid of her daughter.

Sally was the middle child of seven. The eldest, Walter, had had a fight with their father and had subsequently left home. His father had been out as usual spending the dole money and family allowances on drink. His pitiful wife, Amy, was a toothless, scraggy, scruffy sexless individual with an intense dislike for the sexual act because of all the pain and hardship it had brought her.

That day she had cooked what meagre meal she could from the sparse contents of the larder. As usual she put the largest and best helping on to her husband's plate and while she fed the rest of the family, she placed her husband's meal in the oven to keep warm until such time as he deigned to return home. The gas meter under the stairs, ticked ever so slowly, being as hungry as the rest of the household. Then, starved of shillings and florins, the coins of that day and age, it gave up the struggle and stopped the supply of gas to the small terraced house which contained no love. The steamed fish and mashed potatoes laying between two plates got colder and colder.

Fred Wainwright slammed the front door shut and lurched into the hall, making his way to the kitchen to sit at the table, and demanded his meal. He would often laugh and joke with his cronies and refer to his wife as 'Junction two' because she was the Coventry turn-off. There was nothing desirable about her and she would resist as much as she possibly could all his attempts to satisfy his insatiable sexual appetite. He couldn't afford other women, not even the cheapest of the local prostitutes. They were always to be easily found, standing out in all weathers dressed in their skimpy clothes that they thought alluring and enticing to their trade.

They wore mini and micro skirts coming just below the cheeks of their arses, or long skirts split way past their thighs. The less clothes they had on then the better and quicker they could get their business concluded, and get back out on their respective pitches for the next client. Many were in a catch-22 situation. Many on drugs, which helped to make the more seedier aspects of their chosen occupation more palatable being at the opposite end of the scale to the more affluent call-girls who had their wealthy professional businessmen for clients. So they had to work harder for more money to pay for more drugs to help them in their work to get more money for more drugs. They were always willing to do a quick stand-up job in the alley at the rear of the shops for a fiver if business was slow.

Although Fred had an insatiable sexual appetite, it was more important for him to spend his money betting and drinking because these things were not available elsewhere. He was always able to turn to the cheapest and most readily available source for his sexual desires, that of his daughters and his reluctant wife.

With trepidation, Amy placed the meal in front of him, apologising over and over again, attempting to explain and stress that it wasn't hot because the gas had run out. It wasn't her fault that she hadn't a measly coin left in her purse to feed the meter which would have brought the cooker back to life. With his usual drunken rage he threw the plate containing his meal at his wife. The plate caught her a glancing blow on the forehead before crashing to the quarry tiled floor, shattering into hundreds of pieces.

Walter, aged nineteen at the time, had been sitting at the same table reading the local paper, searching the Situations Vacant columns in the vain hope of bettering the job he held at the local garage as an apprentice mechanic. He was unable to suffer his father's behaviour for one second more. He jumped up and punched his father in the stomach with his left fist and on the jaw with his right, sending him sprawling to the floor. If he had expected any gratitude from his mother he was sadly unlucky.

'You fool, what have you done?' his mother screamed at him, rushing to the aid of her prostrate spouse. 'It's all right Fred, he didn't mean it!' she said placatingly.

'Yes, I bloody well did!' yelled Walter. That was when he decided he had had enough. He left home, joined the Merchant Navy and severed all contact with his family.

Of the two sisters between Walter and Sally, Maisey had left home long before Walter and at sixteen had found employment in a Holiday Camp at Skegness. The other sister, Josie left some three months after Walter, having fallen in love with a youth whose family worked with a travelling fair. She moved into his caravan and only saw the remaining members of her family whenever the fair returned for its fortnight on the local common. That left Sally to bear the brunt of her father's behaviour and forced her to assist her mother with bringing up the remaining three siblings.

Mrs Amy Wainwright was a pathetic, weak creature who, ostrich-like, kept her head buried in the proverbial sand and ignored what was happening to those around her and suffered in silence herself. She lived in constant fear of becoming pregnant again, not only for the pain and medical problems childbirth brought her but also for the financial penalties which they could ill afford. Too much money was going on the demon drink instead of the needs of the family. And she was so ignorant and ill-informed in those unenlightened days regarding family planning. Then, the only well-known method of contraception was for the male to take the initiative and wear a condom.

In the main these were only obtainable at the barber's. When you were about to pay for the haircut the barber would say, 'And something for the weekend, sir?' thereby inviting you to purchase a 'packet of three'. In those days they were referred to as French letters. The derivation was from the fact that the first sheaths or condoms were imported from France and the packet's contents were described in French.

They were still regarded as an expensive and unnecessary purchase by the likes of Fred, who could just about afford the price of the haircut. Amy was often at her wits' end whenever Fred demanded his conjugal rights. This was in addition to his incestuous behaviour with his daughters. There was the time she had been rushed to hospital after having inserted a small plastic cup inside herself thinking and desperately hoping it would contain the flow of his semen and thereby prevent a dreaded pregnancy. Come the time to remove it she was unable to and after a few days she became ill with pain as her insides became enflamed. She managed to stagger to the nearest telephone box at the corner of the street and call an ambulance via the emergency system.

Sally, having survived at home until her early twenties, came to a sudden decision to leave home. Being unemployed she had taken what little money she had managed to scrimp and save and hide away from both her parents, and had set off south to London to seek her fame and fortune. When she left the train at King's Cross the first thing she saw on leaving the station was the stairs leading down to the subway and the Underground. She had never been on a train travelling in the bowels of the earth. She was amazed as she looked at all the different coloured routes of the underground map. Where should she go. Close her eyes and stab at the map with her finger? She looked around her: bustle, bustle, and people rushing past all determined to get to where they knew they were going to, all buying their tickets at the booking office or at the automatic machines displaying a fixed price for the destinations that the ticket would be valid for.

She looked around her in bewilderment, feeling very alone for the first time in her life. Then she made the decision. However much small change she had in her purse would determine what price ticket she bought and hence her ultimate destination. Having bought her ticket she found that it did not state any destination and she was still in a quandary as to which of the places displayed on the machine should she go to. So she opted for her first idea; she closed her eyes and rotated her extended finger round three times on the display and then stopped. When she opened her eyes she saw that she was off to West Hampstead. That was how Sally came to be in a bedsit in the north-west of London. She often contemplated why she was living there. Since her one and only school trip, paid for by a sympathetic teacher, to the seaside to Dawlish when she was ten, plus the picturesque scenes of Devon and Cornwall she had seen in the magazines whenever she had visited the doctors, she had always had a longing to reside in the West Country, certainly not where she now found herself ensconced.

Her present bedsit, which had often been advertised as a 'studio flat', was one of two situated at the top of a large Victorian house under the sloping roof of dull grey slates in a road lined with large old plane trees. Owing to the small front gardens, when the trees were in full leaf they tended to keep out the daylight and sunshine. It would have been worse still had the house been on the other side of the street and not faced south, as it did. The flat, being at the top, also had the advantage over the other flats beneath which were more in the shade of the trees. Sally's flat consisted of a sink, of chipped enamel, a small refrigerator, a small cooker and a cupboard, all partitioned off from the main room which housed a single bed, chest of drawers, a wall cupboard, table, two dining room chairs and a small soft armchair. The latter looked as if it had at some time in the past been the habitual resting place for one or two cats. There was also wall-to-wall carpet which was about halfway through its life expectancy, and the room received daylight from a reasonably sized dormer window.

This looked down on to a street, which due to the absence of any garages to the houses, was lined bumper to bumper with cars and vans on both sides, regardless of the time of day or night. No sooner had spaces become available in the mornings, when residents had driven off to their various destinations, so the spaces were eagerly filled by the cars of shoppers or commuters who through lack of parking spaces at their places of employment, parked there and continued their journeys by public transport. It was just as well that Sally wasn't tall, but even at 5' 2" she still occasionally banged her head on the sloping ceilings.

The occupant of the other top flat, Mary Tungate, some two years Sally's junior, worked for a local estate agent. They soon became casual friends, while Sally found a job on the tills in a local supermarket. Although she got on reasonably well with Mary she found her to be very childish and immature and on occasions very catty. Mary would often run Sally down and boast about her possessions and boast how Mummy and Daddy were so good to her. If there was one thing that aroused hatred in Sally towards Mary it was her acute jealousy of Mary's parents. She could cheerfully throttle Mary every time she prattled on about them. Sally and Mary had one thing in common, if nothing else: they had both taken as a means of achieving an income jobs in establishments that were fast becoming available, for the convenience of the public, available seven days a week. Consequently both girls were able to have days off from work in the middle of the week to compensate working the Saturday or on Sundays. So it became a natural progression for them to try and arrange such days of rest to coincide, when they would then spend some time together.

One evening in those days before we as a nation lost our traditional milkman, Sally heard Mary taking her empty milk bottles down to put them out on the front doorstep for them to be replaced with her daily pint of gold top. Sally waited looking over the banister for Mary to return, and as she rounded the last bend to ascend the last short flight of stairs, Sally said, 'As we're both off Thursday how about a day up the West End?'

'Phew, those damn stairs take all the puff out of me!' Mary replied. 'Yes, all right, but I won't take my car; the car parks cost more than the train fare and that's on top of the hassle of driving in town.

That Thursday they took the tube from West Hampstead to Oxford Circus. After they had entered the underground part of their journey at Finchley Road, Mary turned her head to Sally, leaning over until her mouth was only inches away from Sally's ear, and still having to practically shout above the noise of the train as it rumbled through the tunnel.

'Mummy has invited me to dinner on Sunday week, she said I could bring you,' Mary said loudly.

Although Sally wasn't enamoured with Mary and her parents, she would never look a gift horse in the mouth and would suffer anything for a free meal.

'That'd be lovely!' she shouted in reply nodding her head vigorously to reinforce what she was saying. All further conversation was only really possible while the train was in the stations.

On that Sunday morning Sally only ate a very light breakfast knowing that she was going to have the benefit of a main meal reasonably soon as dinner was to be at two o'clock and not an evening meal. Mary's parents lived on their own in a four-bedroomed detached house in Mill Hill, in north-west London. The two girls set off in Mary's car.

'I'd better get some petrol,' Mary said, glancing at the petrol gauge just before pulling into an Esso garage on their left. 'As I've got my flexible friend,' said Mary practically waving her credit card in Sally's face, 'I'll also get Mummy some flowers.'

Sally sat fuming in the car while Mary operated the pump and then went off to pay and purchase 'her precious Mummy's precious flowers'.

She needn't think that I'm going to give her anything towards the petrol and flowers, Sally thought spitefully, she would have got them whether or not I was going with her.

They arrived in good time and Mary introduced Sally to her father who answered the door. He was a thin wiry man with dark receding hairline (he would be bald before much longer). He wore horn rimmed spectacles and had very wet lips where he constantly licked them. He smiled at Sally with practically a leer, looking longingly at her ample breasts, and seemed to hold her hand in the handshake greeting for far longer than was necessary or polite.

Oh my God, not another pervert, thought Sally. She quickly extracted her hand and said hello to Mary's mother, who had come from the kitchen and welcomed her daughter with a kiss.

'Come into the dining room, dinner is ready. I'm just going to serve it,' she said warmly.

Chalk and cheese, thought Sally looking at Mary's parents. Her mother was a plump woman with a round cheery face and an annoying habit of chuckling after every sentence that she uttered, as if it were the punchline of some excruciatingly funny joke. During dinner Mrs Tungate asked Sally what it was that she did for a living.

Before Sally had a chance to reply with some 'vocation' like personal assistant or fashion designer, Mary blurted out, 'She's on the tills in Waitrose!' Once more Sally raged within.

'Such a pity to get stuck in a dead-end job like that,' offered Mrs Tungate. 'Mary is training to be a valuer with an elite estate agent, aren't you, my pet?'

And that's how the conversation more or less progressed all day, somehow deriding Sally while pouring praise on Mary. Sally was quite relieved to get back to the sanctuary of her own little world that evening.

'Darling, get the Waterford Crystal out for the wine, will you?' Sally mimicked Mary's mother as she lay in bed that night. Pretentious old fart, she thought. Though really she was thankful that the conversation had been dominated by and concentrated on the Tungates. This saved her the task of having to invent a past in order not to have to disclose anything about her sordid parents and unfortunate home life.

Some weeks later Sally answered a knock at her door to find Mary standing there.

'Oh hi, come in! I've just put the kettle on, do you want a cup of coffee?' Sally asked.

'Yes please. I've not been in long, the traffic is chaos out there. God knows why I bother to take my car, it wouldn't take long to walk.'

'It would certainly keep you fit, not that we need the exercise with all these stairs every day.'

'Yeah, don't I know it,' Mary replied.

She took the mug of coffee Sally gave her and sat in the soft armchair. Sally took hers and sat on the edge of the bed.

'Anyway what I called for is I've got the chance of a couple of tickets to a rave on Saturday. Do you want to come? It's at a riverside hotel in Richmond,' Mary said.

'Sounds all right, but I'll need to get something decent to wear Saturday morning. If you're off all day we could go shopping together, p'raps to Kilburn?' Sally suggested.

And so it was arranged. Sally already had a decent pleated skirt and so she just wanted a top of some sort to go with it. She had no difficulty in finding something suitable so the shopping expedition wasn't arduous. On the way back they called into the local newsagent's to buy some chewing gum and magazines and while they were in there they each bought a lottery ticket. The rave wasn't due to start until nine o'clock and probably wouldn't get well under way until about ten. It would be an easy journey by train from the British Rail station at West Hampstead direct to Richmond so they planned to set out just before nine.

As they put the final touches to their make-up and donned their respective outfits they switched on the TV that 'Mummy and Daddy' had bought Mary and waited for the Lottery Draw to be made. As the coloured balls dropped one by one into the clear plastic tube they wrote down the numbers.

'I must go and check mine,' said Sally returning to her own flat. When Mary came in a few seconds later, Sally said, ' I might have known it, not one bloody number. I've never had any luck.'

Mary looked at her with a vacant expression. 'Have you got any sherry or vodka or anything? I've got five numbers and the bonus ball!' she announced in a daze.

'I don't believe it, let me check!' said her friend.

Mary was right sure enough. Sally got two wine glasses out of the cupboard and put them on the table.

'Sorry I haven't got Waterford Crystal,' she said sarcastically.

It was an old pine table with drop-leaf sides, only one of which was up, increasing its size by about a third. It was in need of a good scrub or indeed sanding down to remove the scorch mark where someone had negligently left a hot iron flat down longer than was sensible. There were also a number of rings where previous glasses and mugs had left some of their sticky contents to congeal and stain. Sally was about to add to these as she filled the glasses to the brim with Harvey's Bristol Cream, a luxury she allowed herself at weekends.

'Help yourself,' she said to Mary taking up one of the glasses. 'Cheers and good luck!'

They both took a good swig. As they did so Sally thought, I don't know why I'm celebrating, there was no agreement that we would have shared any winnings.

Instead she said, 'I wonder how much you have won?'

Mary shrugged, 'I just picked any old numbers, there's nothing unusual about them,' she declared.

'Yeah, it'll depend on how many others have picked them or worse how many have got five different numbers to you,' Sally replied.

'Still,' said Mary, 'even a couple of thousand won't go amiss; but it's been up in the hundred thousands previously, so tonight's a good night to celebrate, yeah?'

'Sure, let's hit the town. Richmond here we come!'

★

The noise inside the dance hall was deafening. Conversation was impossible. The throb of the bass rhythm and the cacophony of sounds which purported to be music could still be heard across the other side of the Thames flowing darkly and swiftly ebbing, just on high water, towards the sea some fifty miles to the east. The sounds from inside penetrated to the outside in spite of the dance hall windows and doors being closed and heavy curtains drawn to keep out the still cold air of early spring. This, though, was not such a good idea in view of the heat generated by the hundreds of gyrating bodies. Along with the hypnotic affect of the bass beat there was in addition the intermediate flashes of stroboscope lighting in the otherwise dark dance hall making the dancers, for the want of a more apt description, put their movements into slow and jerky motion.

Sally and Mary found that they were among the upper age bracket of those attending. Nevertheless they were both determined to enjoy themselves, Mary the more so. As the evening progressed Sally noticed that Mary was becoming increasingly inebriated. As it wasn't really necessary to have partners on the dance floor, the two girls did not keep that close. As Sally made her way to the toilet Mary spied her and grabbed her arm.

'Hey, I've been looking for you! have one of these,' she said.

'What is it?' asked Sally.

'Ecstasy, sheer Ecstasy,' breathed Mary, and she laughed uncontrollably as she pressed the pill into Sally's hand. 'I'm on my second, wow, I only just recognised you! I'm thirsty, do you want a drink?'

'Not just now, I'll take this in the loo,' replied Sally.

Sally wasn't too concerned when someone barged against her knocking the pill from her hand. It bounced away across the floor getting crushed under the dancing feet. When she came out of the toilet she searched for Mary. The dancing was in full swing now, bodies packed tightly together with just sufficient room for them to move their arms up and down to the beat of the music.

Eventually she found Mary slumped against the wall with a vague expression on her face and an equally vague spotty faced youth groping her with his hand between her legs. He wasn't having much luck as Mary's tight skirt prevented him from penetrating very far. Sally pushed him away and pulled Mary towards her.

'Are you all right?' she asked.

'Jeez, I'm bloody thirsty!' Mary answered.

Sally was aware of the affects of Ecstasy causing dehydration but was also aware of the danger of flooding the kidneys with excess fluid.

'Come on, what you need is some fresh air,' she said, and pushed her friend towards an exit and out into the night.

They soon found themselves on the lawn leading down to the river. Sally walked while assisting Mary, who stumbled as they made their way to the riverside. Mary started to giggle and cry alternately, then gazing at the water said, 'I'm so thirsty I could bloody well drink that lot!'

Suddenly the thought of lottery tickets and thousands of pounds flashed before Sally's eyes. She also remembered all Mary's catty remarks and her precious 'parents', parents that Sally would have loved to have had in spite of their shortcomings. Suddenly she was extremely jealous of Mary. She looked at her standing there unsteady in her drugged and inebriated state.

'Then why the hell don't you drink it, you silly cow of a bitch!' So saying, she gave Mary one hefty shove in the middle of her back and Mary entered the now very fast-flowing river with hardly any splash or noise at all.

'Drink, you catty cow!'

All Sally's hatred erupted like a dormant volcano, re-activated after years of suppression suddenly released into the atmosphere: and hate because she had been constantly reminded of how good Mary's parents had been; hate because of what her father had done to her; hate because her mother had failed to protect her.

Mary was caught briefly in an eddy caused by a protrusion of the riverbank. Sally looked at the five faces staring up at her from the surface of the river. The faces of Mary's parents, the faces of her own parents and Mary's face, all swimming round and round in a whirlpool as she gazed in morbid fascination until they all blended and merged into one, the lone face on the body of Mary.

Sally looked around quickly; there wasn't another soul in sight. She continued to watch Mary floating silently and sinking, floating and sinking until she was suddenly plucked out by the fast current into the main stream of the river where she finally sank without trace. She stared at the dark surface of the water, watching the reflection of the towpath lights, winking and twinkling in the ripples of the water as it rushed on by in its ceaseless journey seawards.

Sally knew that Mary couldn't swim and even if she could she was in no fit state to do so. Sally ran back to the cloakroom, produced her ticket from her skirt pocket and retrieved both her own and Mary's coats and purses. Looking at her watch she decided that she still had time to catch a train home, even if it was the last one to run that night. Getting near the station she started to panic in fear that the train had already left and she sprinted the last hundred yards or so. Her four-inch high heels were not conducive to running, her ankles went over and she was in danger of ricking her ankle. She removed her shoes and carried them in her hand continuing to run in her stockinged feet. She didn't want to be stranded alone in Richmond and ran faster and faster, her breathing becoming painful as she gasped the now cold night air into her lungs. She was getting a stitch in her side and eventually she arrived, out of breath.

She was relieved to discover that the ticket office was still open and that there was a train waiting which was due to pull out in two minutes. As she sat getting her breath back she was pleased that the only other passengers in her carriage were sitting some distance from her. She rummaged through Mary's purse and had a hard time suppressing a shout of glee on finding Mary's lottery ticket. She was even more pleased that Mary had not entered her name and address on the back of it. She leaned back and closed her eyes in bliss sitting there listening to the hypnotic rhythm of the wheels click-clacking over the joins in the rails and gradually dozed off. She felt the train lurch and woke with a start, alarmed as to where she was. The train was just gathering speed and she put her hands to the window to peer into the darkness. She just caught the glimpse of a sign rushing by: Brondesbury. Thank God, she thought, it's the next stop.

The next morning she awoke refreshed and happy with not one iota of remorse. Nothing was troubling her conscience about what had happened the previous night. Without washing or putting on make-up, she went out and bought her usual Sunday Express newspaper. Over her breakfast of tea, two boiled eggs and toast she read that she could expect to receive one hundred and seventy-five thousand pounds for her ill-gotten lottery ticket.

Even she was surprised at having such an appetite. She realised that she couldn't open a bank account while she stayed at that address. Sooner or later Mary's body was going to be found. Would she be reported missing before then? Would she be identified after being in the water for so long? Would she in fact be in the water for long? She expected the police to identify her through dental records and trace her to her parents who would divulge her current address. How long would it be before her parents came to see why they hadn't heard from their darling daughter? They were certainly aware of her own existence. Questions would be asked why she hadn't reported Mary missing. Would it be possible to link them together at Richmond?

Would they suspect me of pushing her in the river? Sally thought to herself. Wouldn't it be better for me to disappear also? Would they think that we were both in the river? Her head was in a whirl. With a possible one hundred and seventy-five thousand pounds burning a hole in her pocket she certainly wasn't going to stay where she was. Yes it must look as if we've both gone missing, Sally concluded.

The next day, Monday, using the payphone in the hall she rang Mary's estate agent and told them that Mary was running a very high temperature and would not be in for the rest of the week. She did the same to her own employer. But she failed to appreciate that that simple act would suggest to any subsequent investigators that they couldn't have both been drowned, unless there was a third party involved.

Sally then let herself into Mary's flat with the key taken from Mary's purse. She hung Mary's coat in the wardrobe, put the key back in the purse, left it on the table and left the flat. At least she was just about to leave and had almost pulled the door closed. She called herself a stupid idiot and rushed back to retrieve the purse. If Mary was in the Thames it was highly unlikely that her purse and key would be behind her locked flat door. The coat, one of many, didn't matter as it was not likely to be traced as the one last worn by her. She would however have to make sure that the purse and contents were disposed of without trace. Best to take them with her temporarily. But take them where? And how? She had always insisted on being paid weekly in cash and didn't have a great deal of money in reserve; certainly nothing in the bank or post office which could be traced to her.

She decided that the best thing was to travel light. One, it would be easier, and two, because leaving most of her possessions behind would add weight to her own 'disappearance'. Luckily she already possessed a fairly large rucksack and a strong plastic and green tartan material grip. Sally packed what she considered to be essential, including Mary's purse, having already transferred all the cash and, of course, that lovely lottery ticket into her own purse. She dressed as warmly as she could, and with a pair of comfortable stout trainers on her feet she set out yet once again to find her fame and fortune – or rather, somewhere to spend her fortune.

She decided that she would travel by public transport to the south-west of London and then try her luck at thumbing a lift. Although she had kept her packing to the minimum she had thought necessary for the expedition she soon found that carrying a grip became tiresome. As she walked between changing buses and the tube she found that she was constantly changing the grip from hand to hand to rest from the weight. The rucksack on her back was more comfortable for travel.

She got off the Piccadilly Line tube at Heathrow, Terminal 4. As much as she would dearly have loved to be able to fly off to some exotic faraway place, she only intended going into the terminal for a snack. With her rucksack and grip she didn't look out of place with all the other many varied travellers, all destined for the four corners of the world. Sally, however, intended to join the A30, the Great South-West Road, to start her hitch-hiking to the West Country.

She hadn't left the terminal building and was still changing her bag from hand to hand as she found the cafeteria. She bought a coffee and a ham and salad sandwich and sat at a table contemplating what she was carrying in the grip. The only really essential items were a few pairs of panties. She transferred these to her rucksack and pushed the grip further under the table. When she had finished her snack, which was to sustain her on the first leg of her journey, she got up and walked out of the cafeteria. She counted the tables as she walked away, one, two, three: she was nearly out.

'Excuse me,' a voice called.

Sally froze in her footsteps.

'Excuse me,' the voice said again.

Sally turned; it was a young man of about her own age. The voice was definitely American and so did his dress appear to be, with a baseball cap, sweatshirt, track-suit bottoms and a pair of trainers that Sally guessed must have cost fifty pounds or more. He was with a girl a few years younger, casually dressed in a short blue jacket and jeans.

The young man proffered a camera to Sally, saying, 'Would you do us a great favour? I've got to leave my fiancée and go back to the States for a few months. Would you take our photo? It's fully automatic.'

Sally agreed, while checking that her bag remained unnoticed where she had dumped it. She took some photos of the couple in different poses and they thanked her profusely when she handed the camera back. She bid them farewell and turned and walked out of the terminal building and out on to the pavement. Nobody called her to tell her that she had forgotten her bag.

★

Now Sally looked warily into the car that had stopped in response to her thumbing, noting Martyn's handsome distinguished face smiling pleasantly at her. She was ready to run or defend herself should the need arise. She had vowed that she would only accept lifts from female drivers. Alas, she had soon discovered that they were very few and far between. She was pleasantly surprised with Martyn's appearance. She had expected some decrepit old fogey behind the wheel, judging from the slow reaction of not stopping until he was well past her; he had had plenty of time to stop sooner, he had only just crawled across the junction. She was well aware of the dangers of hitch-hiking by herself, but circumstances had decreed otherwise. She smiled at the driver.

'Hi, can you give me a lift?' she enquired.

Chapter Three

Ron Baker, PC 697 SW, took his last mouthful of tea and looked at the canteen clock. He had exceeded his allocated forty-five minutes refreshment period by a few minutes. Wouldn't do to take the piss, he thought, although discipline was far less strict and more humane in the job than it had been in his dad's time. His dad had been a typical 'old copper'.

'You youngsters don't know what it's all about,' he'd say, before proceeding to tell them.

In his father's early days whenever they entered the station there was a book, Book 92. All books used in the Met had a number allocated to it denoting its particular use. The most popular book was Book 40. This was just a plain ruled book with a red spine and was used for everything that there was no numbered book designated for, such as booking in and out personal radios or firearms. It was a standing joke. If the Job needed statistics on any matter, then the solution was 'to start a Book 40'. Book 92 was ruled in columns and officers were required to write in the time of entering the station and the purpose of the visit, such as WC or Refs (for refreshments) or Reports, etc. When leaving the station they had to 'bookout' by writing the time of departure. Woe betide any officer found on the station premises without having so booked in, or still in the station having already booked out. They could also be disciplined if the period was considered too long for the particular task in question.

Of course, in those days there had been more discipline in life generally: in families, in schools, and in the forces during and after the war, continuing during National Service. The sergeants and above in the police force of those days having been taught that discipline was the most important task of the rank, they were more prone to checking Book 92 to catch any officer overdue, even by one minute, than they were in taking an active role in the fight against crime. They certainly didn't give advice and assistance to the constables under their command. They had to learn by experience. It was a good thing that some things had changed for the better since the 'good old days'. But the pendulum as far as life in general was concerned had swung too far in the opposing direction, resulting in more crime and crimes of violence as a result of that lack of discipline in life in general.

Ron entered the communications room.

'Are you out now, Baker?' asked the sergeant.

'Yes, Skip,' replied Ron. Sergeants were colloquially referred to as Skip or Skipper, subject to the easygoing nature of the sergeant so addressed. This was a derivation from the oldest section of the Met, the river police known as Thames Division. The sergeant in charge of the patrol boat was obviously the 'Skipper'.

'Take a couple of Misper forms to 98, Priory Road. The owner has lost two of her tenants,' said the sergeant.

'That's very careless of them,' said Ron taking the forms from the appropriate drawer of the forms cabinet. 'Shan't be long.'

Ron made his way to number ninety-eight with the forms and rang the doorbell. Mrs Rachel Goldblum answered the door and peered through the thick lenses of her spectacles perched on the end of her prominent Jewish nose.

'I'm very vurried, they haven't paid their rent already. No one has seen them for over a veek,' she said, with a strong Austrian accent that you could cut with a knife.

Ron took as many details as possible from her and asked to see their flats, after ascertaining that Mrs Goldblum had duplicate keys available. He verified that the tenants were not in residence, dead or alive, and made a thorough search for names and addresses or persons or employers who might be aware of their whereabouts. Being very much taller than Mrs Goldblum and her missing tenants, he constantly banged his head on the sloping ceilings re-awaking a sense of claustrophobic fear as he remembered the last time he had been in such a room.

It had been about 1.30 in the morning one night duty while he was slowly cruising in his patrol car, known in those days as a Panda car. That was because when they were first introduced to assist the ever-decreasing number of men on the beat in their fight against crime, they were small saloon cars, light blue in colour except for the two doors which were white. This means of identification looked like the eye patches of a panda, hence the name.

As he had turned a corner Ron had been flagged down by a man standing on the corner. The man pointed to a house which was on the corner consisting of three stories including an attic room. The side of the property, which contained the front door, which was open, fronted directly onto the footway.

'I can see smoke and it's hot in there!' the man shouted.

Ron called for the fire brigade on his personal radio and entered the hallway with the man behind him. Immediately to the left of the front door was a flight of enclosed stairs leading upwards. Beyond the stairs on the same left hand side at the end of the hall was a solitary door. There was smoke seeping between the top of the door and door frame. Ron put his hand to the door and felt the heat.

'Don't open that door until I've got every one out from upstairs,' Ron told the man as he rushed up the stairs two at a time, shouting as he went for anyone there to get out. He kept running until he reached the top and entered the attic room. It was dark inside with a faint eerie light coming from a small window. He groped around by the door frame and found the light switch. In the sudden glare of the single unshaded light bulb he saw a young girl aged about ten in bed. He grabbed her and made for the stairs and bumped into the man who had followed him.

'Here, take her and get to hell out of here!' said Ron, thrusting the girl at him; she was still fast asleep. He didn't find anyone else as he searched the rooms on the second floor and was then confronted by another man on the stairs.

'Do you live here?' Ron asked him.

'No, I just came in to help,' the man replied.

I wonder, thought Ron, or is he just an opportunist thief taking advantage of the confused situation to help himself to anything of value?

Such things often occurred, unfortunately, in similar circumstances. He would have to give the man the benefit of the doubt; another sorry state of affairs if the man's intentions were strictly honourable and brave. Just then, as a result of the fire services' arrival and their keenness to get at the seat of the fire, they had opened the ground floor room door. A dense cloud of dark grey smoke accompanied by intense heat surged out and erupted up the stairs as fast as hot air was able to rise.

Ron and the man were suddenly engulfed in thick acrid smoke and fumes depriving them of life-sustaining oxygen. Ron grabbed the man's arm and, coughing and spluttering, they crouched as low as possible as they felt their way along the wall and down the stairs. Ron was shit-scared that the whole building, now engulfed with heat and being suddenly supplied with fresh oxygen, would combust at any moment in a fireball. With tears streaming down their cheeks as the smoke penetrated their eyes the two men reached the first-floor landing and Ron thankfully found a window which looked out onto the street. He managed to open it, although it was fast becoming warped with the intense heat. As the smoke billowed out of the now open window, Ron pushed the man out so that he was standing half out and half in with one foot resting on a small ledge just below the window. Ron prayed that the stairs and landing would not burst into flames while he waited for his turn to climb out and down the ladder that the firemen had placed up to the window.

'Officer, officer!'

Ron came back to reality with a start. Mrs Goldblum was speaking to him. 'Officer, ven vill I be abull to let my flats?' she asked.

He thought she might be of German or Austrian extraction. Bloody hell, let the beds get cold first he felt like telling her.

Aloud he said, 'Well, it depends on what contract you have with your tenants, but if they aren't traced within a few days I suppose it would be in order for you to pack their belongings and store them until they are claimed. We'll keep in touch.'

He made his way down and out to his Panda which he had had to park some distance away in the nearest space available. On returning to the nick he passed one NCR copy of the Misper (Missing Persons) report to the controller for circulation and entry onto the Police National Computer and placed the original top copy in Book 56, the Missing Persons binder.

Ron said to his colleague in the communications room, 'Hey Tony, talking of missing persons did you hear about that journalist who worked for *Life* magazine in New York? John Ree was his name, a likeable fellow with a pleasant nature, always punctual, always reliable. One day he failed to turn up for work, failed to make contact and couldn't be found at home. So *Life* magazine hired a private detective to look for him. Well, three weeks passed by and the private eye was about to give up when he walked into a small bar in downtown New York. There sitting dejectedly in the corner drinking a beer was the journalist. The detective walked straight up to him and said, Ah sweet Mr Ree of *Life*, at last I've found you!'

Tony scored a direct hit with a screwed-up ball of paper.

'Get out on your beat!' he yelled, which Ron promptly did.

Chapter Four

Four days after Mary entered the Thames, George Isley, the keeper at Richmond Lock, having eaten well on his usual full English breakfast of egg, sausage, bacon, fried tomatoes and toast, followed by hot buttered toast and marmalade and numerous mugs of tea, went out into the early morning sunshine to greet the first of the river trippers waiting patiently in the lock to go down stream towards Kew. He was a stout, thickset man with a ruddy weather-beaten complexion, who wouldn't have looked out of place in a turtleneck sweater, smoking his pipe while sitting in a rowing boat in the harbour at Polperro, Cornwall.

Having just had breakfast didn't mean that he had not been long out of bed. Indeed, he had been up at the crack of dawn along with all his feathered friends who had been serenading him daily with their dawn chorus ever since he had moved into the small cottage with his wife Patricia. The official hours of the lock were from 8 a.m. until dusk. George would occupy his time until breakfast time in his small garden.

In its setting George decided from the outset that he should obviously have a 'cottage garden' as opposed to a suburban type or architecturally designed garden. He always maintained that not only should a garden be pleasing on the eye, it should also be pleasing to the nose. He ensured that his garden contained lots of lavender, shrub roses, pinks and honeysuckle. He also had what he liked to call his container garden at the nearby lock office. This consisted of window boxes, hanging baskets, pots, urns, tubs and anything else he came across that was capable of containing soil for plants. He even had two old car tyres, one on top of the other, which he painted white, in which he planted bright red geraniums. He also had two large terracotta pots in which he planted tobacco plants which would last until the first frosts of the autumn. He liked the delicious nutmeg-like fragrance that they gave off. But his container plants would have to wait until the danger of a ground frost was over. As a general rule this was about early May.

Just lately there had been a nagging thought becoming increasingly prevalent, which would dominate his every act of life. His beloved cottage and garden came with the job and when the time came to retire he would have to leave it all behind. Still, whenever his old bones creaked as he straightened up having been bent down weeding or tending his plants, he realised that even if the mind was willing his body couldn't cope for ever, and he would be ending his days in a small flat somewhere, with, if he was lucky, some window boxes.

As he was about to go in and wash and shave for the day and have his breakfast, he felt a cold wetness on his hand. He looked down at his faithful friend Jess, his black and white collie.

'Hello me old mate, do you know what I've been thinking?' said George.

Jesse stared back at her master with unblinking eyes. It was uncanny how she knew various different things, such as time. Every morning just a few minutes before George got out of bed to go to the bathroom so Jesse would arise from her basket, lined with some old sweaters of George's, and silently climb the stairs to lie in wait outside the door.

It was also weird how Jesse could possibly know of the silent approach of another dog, cat or fox, which was well out of sight behind the hedge or fence. But she could: her ears would prick up and she would stare at the fence and give a warning bark to let the other know that her side of the fence was her territory.

George had had her since she was a puppy. She would always lie peacefully nearby, surveying all that went on. George knew that he would never have another dog. Nearly all flats had covenants forbidding the keeping of such pets. He knew that he and Pat were destined for a flat in their retirement. It was a godsend, really, that Jesse would see her days out where they were before the time for retirement came. It would have been unbearable to have had to give her to someone else or had her put down.

'Come old girl, let's see if there's a sausage for you this morning,' said George, as he rubbed Jess's ears and her tail wagged nineteen to the dozen. She was getting on also, being fourteen years old.

He knew that Patricia would have a tinge of regret as well. Not that she had ever been one to like gardening. Oh, she loved the garden, yes, but was more than happy to let George get on with it. She would miss the river as well. But she, and thanks to her, George, would have many happy reminders of their life down by the river: Patricia loved to paint. Over the years in the garden and along the river bank and towpath there had been plenty of rural scenes and riverscapes which she had committed to canvas. One day their favourite ones would adorn the walls of their retirement home and fill them with joy and happy memories. George's memories, however, could not all be happy ones.

He hoped he wouldn't have to undergo another incident such as the one that had happened only yesterday. He looked at the quality of the craft assembled and noted without real justification that there were no crews as pretentious as the one waiting its turn yesterday.

There had been a fair amount of trippers taking advantage of the light river traffic in the early season. The launch in question was obviously very new and expensive, all highly polished varnish and brass with, he had realised later, a not very experienced crew. Not that the latter was by any means unusual, as the majority of craft were only hired from one of the many boat yards that lined the Thames. They were nearly always people doing it for the first time.

On this occasion, the rest of the family comprising the crew busied themselves, two standing patiently at the side of the lock, each holding a guy rope from the bow and stern to steady the boat while the water was pumped in to bring the boats up to the level of water on the other side of the lock gates. While they did this, the 'Captain' or elderly head of the family, dressed resplendently in his new sailor's white cap, navy blue blazer and snow white slacks, looking and acting like a right poser, was leaning nonchalantly with arms folded against the small flagpole that stood at a twenty-two and a half degree angle, flying a multicoloured pendant at the rear or stern.

Suddenly there was a loud splintering of wood and the flagpole gave way under the unaccustomed weight pressing against it and both it and the poser fell down into the murky waters of the lock. It would have been quite hilarious in a *Carry On* film, but like many escapades humorous because of the misfortune of others, it was a very serious situation indeed. He wasn't wearing a life jacket, an essential piece of equipment for all river trippers except the most confident of swimmers. Whether he was or was not a good swimmer was of little consequence to George. His concern was that the unintended bather could quite easily be crushed between the boats or lock side or be forced down under their hulls in the confined space of the lock.

Fortunately for all, George was able to bring the man quickly to the side with the aid of a boat-hook which was always to hand. The poser suffered no harmful affects apart from losing his nice new cap, soaking his cherished ensemble, and injuring his pride.

But if George was hoping for a quiet uneventful day today he was another who was going to be sadly unlucky. He pressed the control button to close the lock gates behind the *Blue Maiden* and *Victoriana* both docilely floating broadside to each other prior to the level of water taking them down to that at the other side of the gates ahead of them, in order to allow them to proceed onward towards Kew or Southend should they so wish.

George looked at the indicator which should show him that the gates were fully closed and that he could start the process of pumping. But the indicator still showed that the gates were open. Surely, he thought, the last two boats were fully in the lock and clearing the gates. He confirmed that they were and tried once more. Still the gates were not fully closed; no doubt due to a fallen branch floating there or some other flotsam blocking the way.

It was true that great strides had been taken to clean the river. The Thames was getting cleaner by the year, and there were even reports of salmon being sighted up river. It was going to take a long time, though; there were still rogue and negligent companies caught discharging effluent into the water.

George made his way across the first gate armed with his indispensable boat-hook. He looked down between the gates which were about eighteen inches apart. All he could see was the water lapping gently against the gates. He took hold of his boat-hook and plunged it into the water, just as a punter might have done with his pole some miles further up the river at Eton. The end of the pole came into contact with some unseen object that was preventing the gates from fully closing. What it was George hadn't the slightest idea, but whatever it was, was firmly wedged between the gates. The crews of the craft waiting patiently to be allowed to continue their journey down stream were becoming more anxious to do so.

While they were waiting two children from one of the boats had been feeding their stale unwanted bread to the swans and ducks on the other side of the lock gates. Their mother called them back to the boat.

'Don't run, or you'll trip and fall in the water!' she called.

George retraced his steps to the control panel and having reopened the gates once more, went back to have another look. He still couldn't see anything and was about to plunge the boat-hook back in when he thought he saw a faint blurred image some way down in the murky depths of the lock's water. He gazed down, and the image came nearer and nearer to the surface. As it did so, so it became more clear, as would an image in a pair of binoculars as the lenses were adjusted. George gave an involuntary groan as he realised what it was that he was looking at. There, staring up at him just below the surface of the water, was the very white face of Mary, with unseeing eyes and mouth wide open, her body now released from the grip of the two gates.

Having been a lock keeper for more years that he cared to remember, this was by no means the first body it had been his misfortune to fish from the clutches of Old Father Thames. He was therefore quite familiar and competent with the procedure to be followed. So also were the police. With any lifeless body taken from the river, or anywhere else for that matter, it was their duty to supply the coroner of the district with the evidence to ascertain the cause and circumstances surrounding the death. Was it accidental? Suicide? Murder? Or natural causes? George quickly and discreetly took Mary's body from the water and away from the prying eyes of the shocked boat trippers. George knew the phone number of Richmond police station without having to look at the list of useful telephone numbers displayed by the phone in the office. He dialled the number and set in motion the necessary procedures for the matter in hand.

Detective Inspector Bob Jackson phoned PC Eric Donnerly, the coroner's officer some days after the discovery.

'Morning, Eric, DI Jackson here, has the pathologist's report on the woman we took out of the river last Wednesday been prepared yet?

'It's being typed now. Do you want it put in the despatch?'

'No, give me a ring when it's ready and I'll come and get it.'

The post mortem revealed that Mary's lungs were full of river water, and therefore she was alive when she entered the river and therefore drowned in the Thames. Although the body had various marks and abrasions caused no doubt by coming into contact with the hulls of passing river craft, unseen by the crews, there were no other marks that would have shown that violence had been used against her. Neither was any semen found to suggest that sexual intercourse had recently taken place – although intercourse could have taken place using a condom. There was however no evidence of forceful sexual intercourse indicating rape.

In addition to the river water found in her stomach, the contents also contained a high level of alcohol and the drug Ecstasy. It wasn't necessary to make enquiries to ascertain if there had been a recent function in the neighbourhood where both these latter substances would have been easily available. Last Saturday's night duty relief had been called many times to incidents involving the patrons of the rave at the Regal Hotel. Mary's flimsy attire had suggested that she had indeed attended just such a function and had not been out walking in outdoor clothing.

They had not at this stage identified her, and no one answering her description had yet been reported as missing. Armed with only a post death photograph, which was obviously not as flattering as even the worst passport photograph, they had interviewed the staff at the hotel. Hardly surprisingly, no one could recognise her as having been in attendance. What *was* surprising, though, was the fact that there had not been any outdoor clothing left behind in the cloakroom or elsewhere. It certainly hadn't been warm enough for anyone to travel dressed only as Mary was. She could of course have arrived by car, but again no car had been left in the car park. This was large and free and so the likelihood of a visitor not parking there close to the hotel was remote.

If she hadn't been the driver of the vehicle that brought her to the dance, then why hadn't the driver of any such vehicle raised the alarm when the time to go home came or when returning to collect her? She could have arrived by taxi; if so they would have to see what future enquiries of taxi and minicab drivers would or would not reveal.

Of course, all this was assuming that The Regal was where she had been prior to her death. Bob Jackson was ninety-five per cent sure that that was where she had been, but he had to keep an open mind about it. In any event he set up a murder squad in a small seldom used office on the top floor of the nick at Richmond.

Chapter Five

Rosemary poured herself a glass of dry white wine and took it up to her bedroom and placed it on her bedside cabinet. She slipped off her housecoat and looked at herself in the full length mirror of the wardrobe. Yes, she thought, as she cupped her breasts in her hands and pulled her stomach in, not bad for a fifty-year-old. Plenty of life in the old bitch yet! She climbed into bed and sat propped up by two pillows with the duvet pulled up to her waist. She always became restless at this time. She didn't like being alone at night. She picked up the book that she had been reading but found that reading erotic novels did more harm than good. She slid her hand under the duvet and caressed herself over and below her soft pubic mound. She yearned for the touch of a man.

On impulse she got up, put on her housecoat and went downstairs. She soon found what she was looking for and with the small note book open at the letter 'P' she dialled the number. She knew that she was taking a gamble. They could send anyone, short, fat, bald, ugly or – heaven forbid – a woman. They were beginning to get more women in the Job nowadays.

She put the hall light on and opened the front door. It wasn't long before a Panda car drew up silently across the other side of the road. PC 342 TW, Ted Brooks, handsome, medium build, 5'10", got out and came up to Rosemary.

'You think you've heard someone out the back?' he asked politely.

'Yes, that's right, the back door is through there,' she said, pointing to the kitchen at the end of the hall.

Ted crept silently though to the back door and tried the handle; it was locked and he couldn't see any key. He turned round to ask Rosemary for the key but for a second or two he was speechless. Rosemary was standing at the kitchen door with her housecoat undone and wide open exposing her full frontal self.

'I'm so sorry, I lied. I'm just so terribly lonely,' she said quietly.

That was to be the first of many such clandestine visits that Ted made to Rosemary.

Chapter Six

Ted Brooks wasn't enamoured of what he considered to be 'grotty' Section House accommodation at the rear of Dalston nick. Way, way back in pre-World War Two times, police station areas were divided into sections, each containing so many beats. The sergeant responsible for supervising those beats was the section sergeant. The living quarters of the young (and not so young) unmarried constables was the Section House. The old houses, such as the one Ted was now designated, apart from being, perhaps, freshly decorated, were as archaic as the day they were built.

They consisted of large rooms or areas divided and partitioned off into cubicles of about ten feet by six feet. They were sparsely furnished with a single bed, a locker with drawers and hanging space for clothes, a small table and a square of carpet by the bed. The partitions were only about seven feet high and open from the top to the ceiling. To see and talk to your neighbour you only had to stand on your bed and look over the partition. There was absolutely no privacy and you weren't allowed any radios or television. For that you had to go to the common lounge.

'The sooner I find a bird and get married, the better,' said Ted to his colleague and neighbour the day he arrived. 'I wonder if Gilbert and Sullivan knew about this when they composed *A Policeman's lot is not a happy one, happy one*?'

Neither did he think much of the grimy streets and small shops of the East End to which he was posted as a Probationer PC. Night duty was a bore. Very little in the way of crime happened on his station's ground at night. Local villains didn't 'shit on their own doorstep'. There were much richer pickings to be had in the more affluent areas of the 'smoke'. But woe betide any officer who failed to discover any untoward happening on his beat before booking off duty the next morning. So it was that he was forced religiously to walk the streets shaking hands with all the padlocks and testing doors and windows to ensure that they were all safe and secure.

Night duty became a nuisance and this particular night even more so in view of the six inches or so of snow that had fallen that evening. Ted was cold and miserable and longing to be in a nice warm bed. Crump! He was brought out of his reverie in an instant. Crump! Another missile exploded not six inches from his head. He turned and ducked just as another snowball shot in his direction from the hand of 'Dusty' Miller on the next beat. He was with another colleague who was well off his own beat from the other side of Dusty's. So battle commenced for a few exhilarating moments. At one stage Ted was about to give chase down an alleyway when the Divisional 'Q' Car, the plain-clothes patrol car, drew silently up on the snow-covered roadway.

'What's happening? Need any help?' called the sergeant from the rear of the warm car.

'No, it's all right,' called back Ted, 'my mates just after a drunk and disorderly. Nothing to worry about.'

The sergeant wasn't very impressed, but plain clothes weren't designed for leaping about in the snow so they were quite willing to drive on. The three intrepid snowballers had a good laugh at the situation but decided it was time they all worked their respective beats like good policemen.

Times had now changed. Ted had since married and was buying a small house in Hounslow. He was now stationed at Twickenham. Night duty, though, was still reasonably quiet. Contrary to popular belief, most crime such as burglary and shop breaking were committed in the late afternoon and evenings. One night just before midnight Ted received a call on his personal radio, to call at a private house where the occupier thought there might be suspects at the rear.

Having spoken to and seen Rosemary, he soon realised what was on offer and quickly stopped any back-up arriving; he certainly didn't want any assistance with the task ahead and he radioed the result back that the premises were intact and there was no call for further police action. Well, there was no call for further official police action, but Ted was most willing to assist and satisfy the nymphomaniac Rosemary. These personal radios, thought Ted, are the best invention since sliced bread. He was still able to keep in touch with the nick while being even more in touch with Rosemary.

One Thursday night they were both engrossed, working up to achieving a mutual orgasm, when Rosemary stiffened, blimey that was quick, thought Ted; but he saw Rosemary with her mouth open staring fixedly over his left shoulder. He too then turned to stare in horror.

Chapter Seven

DI Bob Jackson was a stout 5'11" with a thick main of white hair. He had a fresh complexion and always smartly dressed in navy, black or dark grey suits, and was fifty-two years of age. He had been in the Job since he had completed his two years' National Service. He had never regretted his Service life and had enjoyed the majority of it. He had served in the cavalry with a regiment, The Queen's Bays, which was a fully-mechanised tank regiment that had served during the Second World War as part of the Desert Rats. During his National Service he also wore the Divisional flash on his shoulder of the jerboa. A jerboa is a desert rat, which is how the troops achieved their famous name. Although he was in the army for only two years, he rose to the rank of sergeant and had command of his own tank, a Centurion which he still thought was the best tank ever manufactured. Sadly, his regiment didn't exist anymore, having been amalgamated with another regiment, as many others had been in the interests of national economy. He had always intended to ascertain what it had become of his old regiment, but like many other pursuits he had never found the time to do so.

It was one of life's little coincidences that here he was working in Richmond, Surrey, while for the first three months of his National Service he trained with The 8th Royal Tank Regiment at Catterick Camp near Richmond – Richmond, Yorkshire that is. Whenever conversations got around to holidays and travel by sea and air, he would often relate the story that the only time he had been 'seasick' was on the Yorkshire dales.

He was being trained as a wireless operator/gunner and had been taken out for his first experience of mechanised transport. In the very small confines of the tank turret was the Gunner, behind whom sat the Tank Commander. On the other side of the gun's breech was the Operator who was also responsible for loading the gun. They were all claustrophobically crammed in, surrounded by equipment with only inches of space to move in. The heat from the engine and the stench of fumes, coupled with the deafening roar of the engines, were all nauseating in themselves but added to that was the rise and fall as the tank negotiated the humps and valleys in a see-saw motion as it drove around the tank ranges.

It was more than enough to churn even the most strongest of stomachs. Unlike a four-wheeled vehicle, a tank would keep advancing up a steep slope on its caterpillar tracks until it reached its point of balance whereupon the front would then descend rapidly with the rear rising just as fast. You had this see-saw affect over every hump which was as bad as being in a small boat in a rough sea.

He now had three more years to serve in the police in order to retire after thirty years' service. 'Retire' was really a misnomer. Although a police pension was worth working for and was the main prospect that kept officers in the Job till the bitter end, it was not enough to carry on living in the manner police were accustomed to. So it was always beneficial to seek other employment after retirement. No one completely retired on leaving the police force, or 'Service' as the politically correct would now have us call it, unless they had some other means of income. Bob couldn't wait for the day to come when he could at last retire. This was quite general among those of Bob's age and service.

These officers had joined when things were more like *Dixon of Dock Green* of the 'Blue Lamp' fame. Not like now, with drugs and violence with guns and knives and the villain's lack of respect for the 'cloth'. In his early days on the beat, a lone copper, armed with only a whistle and a light wooden truncheon, did not have the comforting means of communication via personal radio. Even so, he was able to walk up to a group of Teddy boys congregating on the corner and say, 'Come on now, lads, home you go,' and they would quietly move on: such was the respect that they had for the uniform.

Bob was sitting one day in the canteen with his usual breakfast of a cup of tea and two slices of buttered toast, having read all the crime reports that had been filled out since he was last on duty the day before. He had assigned them to various DCs and DSs for investigation. He was joined at the table by DC Yvonne MacKenzie who had just returned from the scene of a 'breaking' at a detached house on Richmond Hill.

'How'd you get on, Yvonne?' asked Bob.

'All right, Guv; it's rather a heavy one, I'm afraid,' Yvonne replied.

'What's gone?'

'Mainly small stuff, and a lot that's easily identifiable, thank goodness. Soco's there now splashing powder about. I've arranged for the occupiers to come in for their elimination prints to be taken.'

'Good, so we may get a result then?' said Bob.

'Yes, hopefully when they try to fence the stuff. By the way, I was out your way the other night. I actually drove down your road. There was a Panda parked near your drum, no trouble, was there?'

'Not that I know of, but then I tend not to get too involved with neighbours for that very reason. I get fed up with having my ear bent about all the accidents and traffic offences that they have had, hoping I can do them a favour. They don't seem to realise that they have their own Home Beat Officer and local police station. It's the same as doctors not wanting to disclose their profession at social gatherings. What night was it anyway?'

'Last Thursday, I'd been to the Albert Hall to a Harry Connick Junior concert.'

'Any good?' asked Bob.

'Yes, it was a good night out. Well, I must press on! You can't do enough for a good governor,' she said smiling.

Bob sat for a few minutes more thinking. Last Thursday, he mused, I was on night duty. Alarm bells began to ring in his head.

It was another seven weeks before it was his turn to cover the district for a week as the officer in charge of the Night Duty CID. He waited until the Thursday night before he made his way home at 12.30 a.m. He parked his car some yards away from his house and walked quietly to it passing a stationary and unattended Panda car. He felt the bonnet, it was only warm to the touch and rapidly cooling. It had obviously been there some time. He looked at his front bedroom window and could just make out the glow of the room light burning brightly behind the drawn curtains.

Bob opened the front door quietly and crept silently up the stairs and stood outside his bedroom door. He could hear the headboard banging against the wall. It was a good thing that it wasn't a party wall otherwise the neighbours would be having a good laugh at his expense, if not a troubled sleep. He held his breath as he listened. In addition to the headboard, he could hear the rhythmic pounding of the mattress, the gasps, grunts and sighs as the two bodies within writhed and pushed against each other, oblivious to all else around them.

He walked calmly into the bedroom and noticed on a chair a pile of discarded clothing, folded neatly. Over the back of the chair was a police tunic with chrome numerals and letters on the epaulettes, 342 TW. The pulsating bodies ceased movement abruptly, and first his wife Rosemary looked at him and then the man on top of her looked at him in dismay.

'Get your bloody clothes on and get out, you bastard! Think yourself lucky that I don't kick your teeth down your throat! Nor am I going to make this official, but I'll tell your Duty Officer on the quiet that you are failing to work your beat.' This was an ironic choice of words and even in that situation he strove not to laugh. 'He'll be keeping an eye on you in the future!'

There was only himself and his wife living in the larger than average three-bedroomed semi. His two children had both married and left home. He moved his possessions into the rear bedroom and had had a separate existence from his wife ever since. He was well aware that this was a typical scenario for the force, where shift work and long hours coupled with court attendance and special duties played havoc with matrimonial bliss.

Now once more he was working long hours in charge of the murder squad investigating the death of one Mary Ann Tungate. This could also be linked with the disappearance of one Sally Wainwright, who might also be lying or floating dead somewhere.

Chapter Eight

'Hi, can you give me a lift?'

Martyn leaned forward putting his hand down by his right foot and pulled the lever that released the catch on the boot lock.

'Put your things in the boot and come on board,' he said to her.

When she was seated beside him and had fastened her seat belt she said, 'Thanks a lot!'

He closed her window. 'Where are you making for?' he asked.

'To be honest, I'm not really sure, eventually Devon and Cornwall, I hope,' she replied.

'Well, that's a coincidence, I've no particular destination but I had intended at some time to make for the West Country. My name's Martyn by the way, Martyn Burgess,' he said, turning to her briefly.

Sally was looking out at the passing hedges and green fields and said, 'This must be my lucky day! My name's Janice Stone,' she answered.

Was it his imagination or did she seem to hesitate before saying her name? They exchanged pleasantries and gave their respective reasons for their present situations. Sally, or Janice as she henceforth wished to be known, offered a mixture of half truths and pure fiction. It all sounded most plausible and satisfied Martyn's initial curiosity. He decided that instead of driving aimlessly as he had been, he would now make for a definite place of refuge for the night.

'If it's all right with you, I think we should aim for Shaftesbury and decide what to do when we reach there,' he told her.

'Yes, that's fine by me,' she replied, only having a vague idea of where Shaftesbury was.

As the journey progressed she found herself relaxing more and felt quite comfortable in Martyn's company, feeling that she had known him for much longer than just the few hours that had passed. They found reasonable accommodation in a guest house on the west outskirts of the country town.

'This looks quite a presentable place,' said Martyn as the car's wheels crunched to a halt on the pebbles of the short semicircular drive. 'It will be more convenient and cheaper if we get a double room,' he suggested.

'Oh yeah?' she said cynically.

'Well, we'll try and get twin beds. I believe beds are for getting a good night's sleep! Sex can happen anywhere, any time, what do you reckon?'

'If you say so, but I must warn you that I'm rather off men at this moment in time.'

Janice thought, he's a cheeky blighter, although she had known Martyn only for a very short while she realised that she was becoming quite fond of him and looked on Martyn more as a father figure craving for the paternal love and affection of which she had been deprived of.

I wonder why she's off men, thought Martyn, wishfully thinking there would be plenty of time and opportunity ahead for sex with Janice, and time to find out why she should be off men. Having put their luggage in their room and freshened up, they sat in the lounge while they decided where they were going to eat. Sally noticed that day's copy of the evening paper on a side table. She saw the headline, BOMB SCARE CHAOS AT HEATHROW.

As she picked up the paper she said, 'Look at this, I was there only this morning.'

As she read the report she felt her face going red. It couldn't be true, could it? The more she read the more she realised that it was her abandoned bag that had caused all the panic. Her bag being left unattended, particularly at Heathrow, had been suspected of being an IRA or some other terrorist's bomb. Thank God there was nothing in the bag that could be traced back to me, she thought as she finished reading.

As the conversation turned to bombs, Martyn told Sally how close he had come to being buried under rubble during the war when he was eight years old. He told her where he was living at the time. He was very surprised when she told him that she knew exactly where it was. What a small world it really was! He went on to explain that at the rear of his house it was completely open for quite some distance, being railway sidings and goods yards.

One day, he couldn't now remember if it was in the morning or afternoon, he knew that he was alone in the house; his father was obviously out at work, his mother and sister may have been out shopping. He could remember standing in the passage between the lounge (or front room as they used to call it) and the kitchen. He felt a tremor and as he looked at the wall it leaned forward right over him in a concave shape. It poised there for what seemed ages but could only have been for a second or two, and then settled back into its original position with not a speck of dust to show what had happened. He was to learn later that it hadn't been a bomb that had been dropped but what was called a landmine which had been dropped by parachute onto the railway sidings.

There being nothing between the site of the explosion and the house the blast wave had carried across, rocking the house on its foundations. Looking back Martyn realised that his house had been pushed over almost to the point of no return and had it continued to go over it would have come tumbling down on top of him. It was mysterious how such a solid mass of concrete and bricks could bend and retract in such a flexible manner.

That first night, after a spaghetti bolognese in a small Italian restaurant, they were preparing for bed when Janice turned to Martyn saying, 'I've got a confession to make. Tarrah!' And she took hold of her fair curls and pulled them away to reveal black short hair.

'My, my, you actually look younger, more impish. I like it very much,' said Martyn.

'Well in that case I'll have to leave it off for a while. In fact I haven't had it off for quite some time,' she said with a twinkle in her eye; but she secretly wondered if it had been sensible to disclose her true appearance.

The daylight hours were beginning to get noticeably longer as they made their way through Dorset and on towards Devon. British Summer time had been in force for a few weeks.

'Martyn, are we going anywhere particular today?' Janice asked.

'Not really, anything in mind?' he replied.

'When I was a kid I went on a school trip to Dawlish. Are we anywhere near there?'

'I'll check the map,' he said. Having done so he told her, 'Well, it's about eighty or so miles, so we have plenty of time and we can rekindle your childhood memories all day tomorrow.'

And so they did, visiting Dawlish Water and The Lawn with its miniature gardens with cascading waterfalls and the Australian black swans. Janice had had such a lovely day and was so happy and carefree that night that she gave no thought to her clothes and belongings. These lay scattered over her bed while she showered prior to going down for their evening meal in the hotel that they had booked into.

Martyn hadn't meant to pry but his attention was drawn to the two purses. One of them was the flat fold-over type with compartments for plastic credit cards. As it lay open it was displaying its contents. He saw the name *Mary Tungate.* He picked it up and found a driving licence in the same name with an address in West Hampstead, London.

Well I'm damned, it's a small world! No wonder she knew exactly where I used to live, he thought. He quickly gave in to the temptation and looked in the other purse. There he found a library ticket in the name of Sally Wainwright of the same address. There was also a lottery ticket carefully preserved in a compartment of the purse. He knew women were inclined to keep all manner of rubbish, barring the kitchen sink, in their purses and handbags. He was sure however that this didn't apply to Janice, who was travelling light.

Why should anyone continue to carry about with them a lottery ticket so carefully? The normal reaction is to screw it up and throw it away as soon as you've discovered that it is not a winning ticket. Martyn had a lot to think about while he was getting showered and ready to go down.

How strange that she had lived in West Hampstead, so near his birthplace. West Hampstead! Yes, he could remember walking with his mother all the way from

Finchley Road, through West Hampstead and on to go shopping along Kilburn High Road. If he was very lucky his mother might buy him a few sweets. He could remember that along the whole length of the road there would be barrow after barrow of costermongers selling their fruit and vegetables and other wares cheaper than the shops because of their low over-heads. Now you weren't allowed to let a vehicle stand for a second causing an obstruction, never mind selling from a stationary barrow, although he was aware that this was still allowed in North End Road, Fulham, and a few other streets.

As they made their way down to the restaurant for their evening meal, he held back under the pretence of making sure that the room door was properly closed and locked. When Janice was just a few stairs down he called out to her, 'Sally!' Janice stopped in her tracks and turned towards him.

As soon as she did so she realised her mistake. The blood rushed to her face making her blush profusely. It then just as quickly drained away, turning her ashen as she stared at him.

'Wha'-what, Ha-how'd you…?' she gasped.

'Would you have reacted the same if I had called out "Mary"?'

She collapsed, sitting on the stairs with her head in her hands. A maid, in her smart black pleated skirt and snow white blouse was coming down the stairs from the floor above and on seeing Janice she stopped looking most concerned.

'Is madam all right?' she enquired.

'She'll be all right, I'll get her a glass of water when we get down to the restaurant,' said Martyn.

The maid seemed relieved at not having to get involved and carried on down the stairs.

Martyn said, 'Do you want to talk or eat first?'

She shook her head, 'I'm not hungry.'

'Well I am, I'm afraid. You'll just have to sit with me while I eat. Anyway you look as though you could do with a stiff drink!' Martyn told her.

The waiter showed them to a fairly secluded table for two in the corner and gave them the menu.

'The wine list is at the rear, sir,' he said.

'Thank you. We would like two Southern Comforts with ice while we're deciding.'

The drinks arrived and Martyn said, 'Are you sure you don't want to eat?' She shook her head. He took a sip from his glass and nodded to hers, 'Well get that down you, my girl, and start telling me all about it.'

Although her drink was only a single measure it was consumed quickly on an empty stomach and with the aid of a second drink it soon loosened her tongue. She related the whole story, breaking off whenever the waiter was in attendance. Afterwards she was amazed and frightened that she had divulged the whole sordid story, although she felt sure that Martyn would not call the police. Martyn was staggered. He quite expected a scenario involving theft and possibly tax evasion or benefit fraud, but murder! That was hard to come to terms with.

The next morning Janice discovered that Mary's purse and the lottery ticket were missing.

'You bastard!' she screamed. 'What have you done with them? You've got them, haven't you?'

'Relax, calm down. I really think they're much safer with me don't you?' Martyn replied.

'Give them back to me, they're mine!' Janice shouted.

'I think that if Mary were here she'd dispute that remark. So what are you going to do about it, call the police? I'm quite willing to share with you, I think it's only fair that you be willing to share with me,' he said calmly.

They had just had breakfast, Janice being ravenous after her fourteen hour or so fast and they were repacking in order to move on. By the time they were ready Janice had regained her composure and was now resigned to going along with Martyn, certainly for the time being. The overnight rain had cleared away and the weather was now starting to get warmer and daffodils were in full bloom everywhere. The glorious bright whites, pale and deep yellows contrasted with the bright green of the leaves and stalks, heralding that first fresh breath of spring.

They drove towards Teignmouth, but had they been normal tourists they would more than likely have carried on to visit Torquay. Martyn, however, had other thoughts brewing. Leaving Teignmouth he kept north of the river Teign, going towards Kingsteignton, then Chudleigh Knighton making for Dartmoor Forest.

He said, 'How about a picnic?'

'Bit cold for that yet, isn't it?' Janice remarked.

'We can always sit in the car and eat. There won't be any cafés about on the moor,' replied Martyn.

Passing through a small village he spied a vacant parking space in front of a small war memorial honouring the dead of the First and Second World Wars. As he pulled in, he said, 'How many I wonder really do remember the fallen heroes in this day and age?'

'I certainly don't, it was all just history for me at school and history certainly wasn't one of my favourite subjects,' said Janice.

But he remembered; or rather he remembered the Second World War which had affected more than the fallen servicemen. He remembered the frightening bombers flying overhead; the crump, crump noise of the anti-aircraft guns that were set up on any convenient spare patch of ground; the thousands of rounds fired into the night sky with little hope of actually hitting any aircraft. What would have happened if they had? Brought the whole lot screaming down to explode with even more devastation on the innocent below?

He had a slight remembrance of being told that the purpose of it was to frighten the Luftwaffe into flying higher and so spoil their bombing aim. It was also a great morale booster for all Londoners and the inhabitants of all the other towns and cities who were suffering the same fate to actually hear that the country was fighting back. He remembered going out with his friends searching the streets for shrapnel, the cruelly sharp jagged edged pieces of blue-grey metal, the remnants of the exploded shells which rained down from the heavens above during the anti-aircraft barrages. It was a wonder that there wasn't more injury and devastation caused by it than anything dropped by the enemy.

He also remembered the bombed garages in Canfield Place and realised ruefully that the threat of death wasn't restricted to war and conflict. Before the war Martyn and his friends were allowed sixpence, that was two and a half pence in decimal currency, to go to the local cinema on Saturday mornings. The afternoons were utilised for the re-enactment of the morning's entertainment. On the other non-schooldays and evenings they would play cricket and other ball games at the far end of the cul-de-sac in the relative undisturbed safety of the mews. Inevitably the ball would end up on the flat roof of the single story garages that were destined to be demolished by the enemy.

Martyn's father had forbidden him to climb up the drainpipe, like his friends, in order to retrieve the ball. Martyn couldn't recall why he had been so banned, but had a vague idea that it was so he wouldn't scuff or damage his shoes in so climbing the drainpipe and therefore hastening the need for the costly replacement of such shoes. As with all little boys aged six or seven, the temptation to do the same as one's mates was too great and one summer evening when their ball went up on the roof, Martyn decided that it was time he ventured forth to retrieve it.

He was no sooner on the roof with the ball in his hand when he was assailed with shouts of, 'Martyn, your dad's coming.'

'I don't believe you, he isn't!' Martyn called back.

'He is, honest!'

The fear of being caught out up on the forbidden roof disobeying his father overwhelmed him. He looked frantically for somewhere to hide. He didn't have the sense to just lay flat out of view. He went to the rear of the roof where there was a foot-high brick wall guarding a sheer drop of about fifty feet to the railway line at the bottom. Visions of his cinema cowboy heroes hanging from such precipices by their hands flooded his thoughts. He was just about to go over the one-foot-high wall and imitate his heroes' actions, little realising that his little hands would not support the weight of his body for long whereupon he would inevitably plunge to his death below.

Luckily an elderly resident in a house on the opposite side of the mews overlooking the garages saw what was about to happen and shouted to Martyn to come away from the edge. Martyn didn't realise until many years later just how close he had come to death yet again. He didn't think his father did, either.

Yes, he remembered, but not so much of those poor sods named on all the memorials throughout the land. If he didn't actually think of them, then what chance was there of the youth of today doing so? Especially when at times it seemed that so many of them were selfish, greedy and suffered a lack of drive to do anything for themselves. They seemed to expect as a right their televisions, videos, personal computers and designer labelled clothing. Many seemed so ready to beg, so willing to live in cardboard cities, so ready to take drugs.

If, heaven forbid, there should be another world war or a war threatening the British Isles, how many would gladly volunteer to fight and lay down their life for Queen and Country?

Blimey, I'm getting old bitter and twisted, he thought. Aloud he said, 'Let's go and buy some rolls, butter and cheese, etcetera, etcetera, etcetera. You have I trust seen *The King and I*.'

'Oh yes, Yul Brynner wasn't it?' replied Janice.

'That's it. Shall we dance? Or shop?' asked Martyn.

They found the village store where they were able to buy all their needs, including a knife with which to cut the rolls and cheese and spread the butter. Janice looked at the knife and the way Martyn was holding it. She shivered; it wouldn't have looked out of place in a butcher's but here and now her stomach turned over just looking at the razor sharp pointed tip.

'That's a vicious looking weapon,' she remarked.

Martyn looked directly into her eyes. 'We need a good sharp knife to cut the rolls,' he told her as he rubbed his thumb gingerly over the edge of the blade. But he thought to himself, yes, it was a very vicious weapon.

Once on the National Park they saw signs to Widecombe in the Moor. It was he knew a very popular tourist attraction. And Uncle Tom Cobley an' all, he thought. No thank you, somewhere a little more secluded and remote for our picnic I think.

They drove along a quiet lane ending up at Becky Falls where they saw the Becky Brook leaping and plunging seventy feet down a series of great boulders. They continued on and found an isolated track where they could see in the distance Bowerman's Nose, an outcrop of weathered rock in that distinctive silhouette to the south of Manaton. They parked off the track on a patch of hard stony ground to have their picnic. They sat in the car with the windows down, watching the shadows of the passing clouds creeping insidiously over the Moor like encroaching hoards of ravenous locusts.

'The best thing about eating alfresco at this time of the year is the absence of wasps and flies,' he said pushing his seat back and turning towards Janice, 'pass the shopping over.'

It was desolate where they had stopped, not another soul in sight, Martyn sat there, knife in hand cutting the bread rolls and buttering them. He passed one to Janice to put the filling in and looked into her face. Had he really contemplated using the knife for a different purpose? Was one hundred and seventy-five thousand pounds sufficient reward for such a nefarious act?

Yes, he thought, it probably was, but that would not be the best way to go about it: far too messy, and too many traces left for forensic science to discover. It was also too gruesome for him. It would be better to get her to the rear of the car under some pretext of getting her to go to the boot for something and then quickly reverse over her. Wouldn't it also be divine judgement for her confessed sins? Maybe, but he was having second thoughts as to whether he should be the one to carry it out. Surely all he had to do was leave her and go on alone; she could hardly raise any alarm. Perhaps when he tired of her he could think again.

'Are we moving on?' she asked as she packed the remains of the picnic away.

'Yes, we might as well. Talking as you were of history, what do you know of Raleigh and Drake?' he asked.

'Oh God, not another lesson! Well, I know Drake finished his game of bowls before knocking seven different colours of shit out of the Spaniards,' Janice replied.

'What a lovely turn of phrase you manage to use,' Martyn ventured.

'Yes, and I know that Raleigh laid his cape over a puddle for the first Queen Elizabeth to walk on, and no I didn't think he invented the bicycle.'

'Well, that just about sums up your knowledge of two of our greatest seafarers. It was from Plymouth that they set sail as did the Pilgrim Fathers in their ship the *Mayflower*. Plymouth also got the shit knocked out of them, as you would poetically put it, by the German bombers in the war.

'Yeah, so did Coventry,' Janice remarked.

'You know Coventry, do you?' asked Martyn quickly.

'No, not really,' she said, automatically denying the truth.

'Well I think a place that has been a naval base since the sixteenth century is worthy of a visit, don't you?' Martyn suggested.

'Plymouth Hoe yes, your puns are catching,' she giggled.

Having had a change of heart and a lack of evil intent, not now requiring solitude Martyn drove down into Widecombe in the Moor, then onward past Two Bridges. Although it's an all male residence, Janice shivered noticeably as they passed close by Dartmoor Prison at Princetown. They then joined the A386 and drove into Plymouth.

'We must get some petrol at the next garage we come to. Pity we're not near a superstore, it's usually cheaper there,' said Martyn.

'Well where ever you do stop, I shall want to use the toilet. Ah, there's a Shell sign up ahead,' Janice told him.

'I've just seen it,' said Martyn switching his offside indicator on and coming to a rest on the crown of the road. When the oncoming traffic had cleared he turned right on to the forecourt and pulled up at the pump nearest the exit. While Janice went off to find the toilet, Martyn filled the tank up. He walked slowly round to the driver's door. Nobody appeared to be paying any attention as he got in. There was no sign of Janice. He switched on the ignition and started the engine. Still no one paid attention, still no sign of Janice.

He accelerated away letting the momentum of the car slam the door shut as he turned left onto the road, narrowly missing a farm labourer laboriously pedalling his bike against the wind. He didn't know what the man called him, but he saw him in the mirror shaking his fist in the air.

Janice emerged from the toilet and browsed around the shop's shelves of confectionery, books, pot plants and motor spares. She was expecting Martyn to enter at any time to pay for the petrol. Then she realised she had been in the toilet and freshening up her make-up longer than she thought. Martyn could have already paid and be waiting outside. She went out of the shop and then noticed the empty space at the end pump where the car and Martyn should have been. It was empty and the car was no where in sight. She looked towards the air pumps but he wasn't there either.

'The rotten shit, he's left me,' she wailed, and felt the tears begin to swell in her eyes.

Martyn found himself driving towards Tavistock. He laughed out loud, he couldn't believe his eyes, there in front of him was a Range Rover with a personalised number plate, J 4 JAN. If she could only have seen it she would have loved it! She wasn't all bad, he thought. Good grief was he actually missing her? And so soon? He saw the brake lights come on on the vehicles ahead. He then saw the reason for this as he brought his speed down to the required 40 m.p.h. limit in force on that section of road. Then he saw the advance warning signs that there were police speed cameras in operation.

'Cameras,' he mused, 'cameras, videos.' His hurried departure and non-payment would be well and truly recorded on the video camera at the petrol station.

As soon as he was able he did a U-turn and hurried back. As he drove in he saw Janice standing alone, forlorn, with tears streaming down her face. As he stopped beside her a look of utter relief flooded over her and her mouth twitched into an involuntary smile of gratitude. Martyn got out and put his arms around her and gave her a kiss, tasting the saltiness of her tears.

'Get in, I'm just going to pay for the petrol,' he said gently.

A Fiesta was now stationary at the pump Martyn had used. The female driver was getting frustrated as she continually squeezed the nozzle handle trying to get the petrol to flow. Nothing would happen until it was cancelled by the attendant in readiness for payment of the amount recorded. Martyn rushed into the shop.

'I'm very sorry,' he said disarmingly, 'I'm in such a hurry I rushed out forgetting to pay.'

Nothing more was said and Martyn drove off, this time in a much more sedate manner, and turned right. Janice, being overwhelmed once again of genuine paternal love suddenly felt a yearning need for the love and affection that Martyn could give her.

'Please Martyn,' she said, 'don't you ever do that to me again!' She put her hand on his thigh and snuggled close to him feeling relieved and comforted, but there was still a tinge of resentment lingering in her sub-consciousness.

'All right, my love,' he said. He in turn stroked the inside of her thigh but had to withdraw it quickly in order to negotiate a sharp right hand bend. Although Janice enjoyed the brief warmth of Martyn's hand, she was glad when he removed his hand, still haunted by the evil actions of her father.

One afternoon they were sitting on a wooden seat by The Dome overlooking Tinside open-air swimming pool which had not yet opened for the summer season. The seat had on the backrest a metal plaque proclaiming the seat to have been donated to the gardens of Hoe Park by a Mr and Mrs Roundshaw in loving memory of their beloved son Trevor, who lost his life in the Falklands conflict. It was another fine day and the sun was warm whenever the cloud allowed it to penetrate through. They were both contentedly licking ice creams. At least Martyn was. Janice aka Sally was not quite so contented. Deep and treacherous thoughts were permeating her troubled mind. Her recent transgression with Mary had been an act carried out without premeditation, but the end result was just as rewarding; at least it had been, until fate had come into play once more. She would now have to be content with as much of the winnings as Martyn chose to let her have. Now it was necessary to plan and premeditate. I don't suppose, she thought to herself, there will be any chance of getting him drunk and pushing him over a cliff or into the sea…

'Penny for your thoughts,' offered Martyn, bringing Janice back from her daydreaming to choke on her ice cream cone biscuit.

'My thoughts are worth infinitely more, much more than a penny. I might tell you for one hundred and seventy-five thousand pounds, though,' she said slyly.

'No chance, I told you, fifty-fifty is a very fair arrangement,' retorted Martyn.

Janice went back to her evil thoughts, dismissing one after the other, knives, blunt instruments and poisons, and shivered.

'That ice cream has cooled me down and the sun has gone in,' she remarked.

'Okay, lets perambulate and find a cosy pub for a bevvy before eating,' suggested Martyn.

Darkness had fallen suddenly, with heavy dark rain clouds blowing in from the sea, and soon the roads and pavements were awash, making people scurry for dry shelter, some protected by umbrellas which were often in danger of being blown inside out by the strong wind. They eventually pushed open the bar door of The Pilgrim Fathers. Although the glass of the door was etched in an ornate design proclaiming the interior to be the Public Bar it was clear on entering that there was no longer any distinction between the quality of the bars. They all had the same plush red and gold pile carpet over the floors, with red leather stools and chairs. Behind the bar was a blackboard announcing the menu of the day in addition to the standard curries, flans and quiches.

They decided they would have a pub meal after their drink that evening. It was obvious from the looks of the others that they were not sure whether Janice and Martyn were father and daughter, man and toy-girl, or girl and sugar daddy. They were both very careful not to give any clues as to their relationship.

The next day, having driven out, they returned through Saltash and over the road bridge spanning the Tamar. The bridge ran parallel to Isambard Kingdom Brunel's Royal Albert Railway Bridge completed in 1859.

'They don't make them like that these days,' said Martyn as they made their way back to the east side of Plymouth. 'What will our present day structures be like in the year 2135 or so?'

They parked in a small pay-and-display car park and partook of a cream tea in a dainty little restaurant with crisp green and white check table clothes and green chairs. Hanging on the walls were framed watercolours of local scenes painted by local artists. Each one bore a price ticket inviting customers to purchase them. After their cream tea, walking into the car park, Martyn was tossing his car keys up into the air and catching them. On the third throw or so he failed to catch them on their downward journey and they fell to the ground.

He stopped Janice in her tracks and looked at the empty space where his car should have been. He looked quickly around the car park in the hope that he had made a mistake about its location, but no, that was where it should have been standing waiting for their return.

'Bloody hell, it's been nicked,' he gasped.

Chapter Nine

Detective Sergeant 'Dick' Turpin, christened Arthur in vain by his hopelessly desperate parents, who knew full well that he would be called 'Dick' by all but his close family, put the phone down and went in search of the DI. He found him in the front office talking to the Late Turn Relief Inspector.

'Guv, I've just had a call from the Devon and Cornwall Constabulary. They've just recovered a stolen car and they think you may be very interested in talking to the loser when he goes to collect it.'

★

Earlier that day, Brian Mould, born some eighteen years earlier in Plymouth, walked into the car park and had a good look around at the array of vehicles parked there. He eventually strolled over to a Toyota saloon he found in the far corner. He was unobserved as he placed an old sparking plug against the rear passenger door window and hit it hard with a brick. It was astonishing how easily the safety glass shattered, and in relative silence, too. The brick he was fortunate enough to have found nearby. Having gained entry through the broken window, he unlocked the driver's door and used the brick to smash the steering lock on the steering column. He cross wired the ignition under the dashboard and the engine spurted into life.

He was enjoying himself driving around until at last he came to halt in traffic in Exeter Street. He was supposed to be out looking for employment but he was fed up with the constant questions and interviews only to receive the stereotype reply of, 'thank you for your interest, but no thank you'. When the traffic moved off in front of him he eagerly lifted the clutch pedal. Too eagerly, in fact, because he stalled the engine. Flustered, he tried to restart it but couldn't. Brian looked nervously around in frustration, sure that any moment someone would notice the smashed window. He panicked and ran off down past the post office at St. Andrew's Cross and on into Old Town Street entering the pedestrian precinct un-pursued.

He had not been wearing gloves. The spring weather was too warm for such apparel. Had he done so, he would have stuck out like a sore thumb and would have looked most suspicious. So though he had obviously left his fingerprints behind, particularly when he adjusted the rear-view mirror, luck was with him. As he had never committed any crime before, let alone been caught and convicted, his fingerprints were not on police records and they would be unable to trace the crime to him. It was his first transgression against the law, and with his heart beating the retreat, he thought it could well be his last.

Having caused further chaos to the traffic situation the abandoned car was removed to police headquarters at Charles Cross. On checking the property in the car, the police found two purses. In addition certain items were also found bearing the names of Mary A. Tungate and Sally Wainwright, both of the same address in West Hampstead, London. The Police Gazette gave details of a case of sudden death involving the said Mary A. Tungate, found drowned in the Thames in suspicious circumstances. It named the officer in charge of the enquiry as DI Jackson at VR Richmond, Metropolitan Police. The Police Gazette also gave details of a Missing Person named Sally Wainwright from an address situated in the Metropolitan Police district of West Hampstead SW. Detective Constable Bryce Jones got up from the computer monitor and having explained the situation to his Inspector got his authority to telephone the Met.

Chapter Ten

Douglas King walked slowly between the rows of stacked metal shelves, all neatly labelled clearly identifying the contents that could be expected to be found there. At the head of each row there was a neatly typed index indicating what items were stored in that row. Douglas had organised the stores in this way many years previously and it could not be bettered to this day. It was, he thought, just like a library but instead of books he looked after all the items necessary to keep a fleet of coaches operating and properly maintained. He not only looked after the needs of the engineering staff but also the stationery requirements of the office staff.

I wont be doing this tomorrow that's for sure, he thought: another day, another life.

He had mixed feelings about his future. Tomorrow nice words would be said about him and he'd be presented with his carriage clock in honour of his forty-odd years of faithful service and then he'd go home. Home to his wife Brenda. They had planned to augment their income by opening their portals to the tourist trade by offering Bed and Breakfast. He felt somewhat guilty about the venture because he realised that most of the responsibility would fall on Brenda's shoulders.

Not that he wasn't capable of cooking the usual egg and bacon and helping with the cleaning. As things transpired, it all worked out well initially and poor old Douglas would never know the difference. The problem only arose last February. After forty years in the storeroom of H.R. Coachworks (Plymouth) Ltd, Douglas King had risen to Chief Storeman and he had taken early retirement when the firm had been bought out by a major competitor.

'After forty years Doug, it's not a great pension is it? Will we manage until we get the state pension?' Brenda asked.

'Yes love, we'll be all right. We've got three unused bedrooms upstairs and we're in a good locality for Bed and Breakfast,' said her husband reassuringly.

To ease the burden of the daily cooking of breakfasts they often indulged in the occasional evening takeaway. They were fortunate in having a good quality fish and chip shop quite near to them. One such evening they enjoyed the meal with fresh crusty rolls and butter.

'I can't manage all this, dear, do you want some?' Brenda asked.

'Yes please, I can always find room for it when it's so delicious,' Doug replied.

The empty plates were cleared away and placed in the dishwasher. 'I forgot to mention it earlier, dear but they need a fresh toilet roll up stairs, before you get settled in your chair for the evening,' Brenda announced.

'No trouble, love,' replied Douglas, thankful that she hadn't waited until he was actually seated. He ran up the stairs with a toilet roll in each hand. He only got as far as the first bend in the stairs when he clutched his chest, gasped, 'Indigestion!' and fell back down the stairs he had just ascended.

He was dead from a massive heart attack before he reached the bottom. And so he came to leave his wife to carry out their plans on her own. She was always worried and apprehensive about her boarders. Her daughter June was also concerned for her safety.

'Mum,' she would say, 'you don't know who you're inviting into your home.' She didn't want to frighten her mother by suggesting that they could well be criminals or homicidal maniacs.

Mrs King would reply, 'I know your offer of your back bedroom is very good of you but I like my independence and the income is very welcome until I'm old enough for the State pension.'

Today Mrs Brenda King of the Plymouth Hoe Guest House knocked on the bedroom door of room number three. It was her only double room.

All alone. And now she worried once again. Although her boarders appeared to be the innocent victim of crime she still didn't relish the idea of the need to be involved with the police. She had been rather doubtful when, after showing them the room, they had stated – or rather *he* had stated as he had done all the talking – that they had no luggage and had given a hard luck story of having had it all stolen. Was it likely?

He had assuaged her fears somewhat by suggesting that she was free to call the police to confirm it. In fact he had asked if he might be permitted to use her phone, in her presence, in order to let the police know that he now had a temporary address at which he could now be contacted.

Douglas had always intended to have a pay phone installed before he had been so cruelly taken from her. She really must get one fitted, she thought. She let Martyn use her phone and now not thirty minutes had passed before she had answered the telephone to an official-sounding person who asked to speak to a Mr Burgess. Janice heard Mrs King's timid knock at the door and opened it.

Mrs King said, 'I think it must be the police on the telephone asking for Mr Burgess.'

'Oh thank you,' Martyn said, pushing past Janice and followed Mrs King downstairs. Yes, they had recovered his car with some minor damage, and although it was not driveable, would he kindly attend the station to formerly identify it and arrange for its collection by a repairer of his choice.

Janice didn't want to go anywhere near a police station so Martyn went on his own. He entered the reception area and waited patiently while a youth with a crew-cut hairstyle and a silver circle earring raised the roof, ranting and raving because his car had been towed away from a yellow line and hadn't they anything better to do, why weren't they spending their time catching criminals instead of picking on the innocent likes of him?

At long last the civilian station officer's assistant called him over to the counter and asked if she could be of assistance. He said she could and that they had recovered his car that had been stolen.

'One moment please, sir,' she had said before disappearing into a room at the rear of the office from where a few seconds later a uniformed sergeant appeared.

'Mr Burgess? Would you come through that door please,' said the sergeant.

He pointed to the door at the end of the counter while he bent down and pressed a button. There was a buzz and a click and the security lock on the door was released and Martyn was able to push it open and enter.

'Come this way, sir,' the sergeant said and led the way to another room. Although Martyn didn't know it at the time, he was in fact placed in the detention room. 'Just wait here a moment,' he was told.

Before Martyn could make any comment the sergeant had left securely closing the door after himself. It was then that Martyn noticed that there was no handle on the door. A minute or so later the sergeant returned with a constable and he was escorted to the charge room.

'Mr Burgess would you please empty your pockets out and put the contents on the table,' asked the sergeant.

Martyn felt the room begin to swim, his stomach churned nauseatingly, and he felt bile start to rise in his throat. He swallowed quickly, 'What on earth for?'

'As a result of some items found in your car, you are being detained until an officer from the Metropolitan Police attends to interview you.'

It wasn't until about 3.30 a.m. that Martyn flopped exhausted onto the rubber mattress, upon which many smelly intoxicated vagrants had lain before him, on the solid hard bench that served as a bed in the cell to which he had been transferred after being searched. The cells of police stations had no respect for class distinction; they were the same for drunken vagrants as they were for well-to-do businessmen detained on thousands of pounds worth of fraud charges.

He succumbed to a shallow and restless sleep. He was brusquely aroused just after eight and offered soap and water from a small basin situated at the end of the cell passage. There was no chance of course of using any such dangerous item as a razor. He dried himself with difficulty on the roller towel, which was nearing the end of its current life cycle, so that the loop became progressively smaller with each subsequent pull. He hardly touched the sausage, beans and egg that they had given him to eat.

'You don't know when you're well off,' said the young constable who was the gaoler for that morning. 'It's the same grub as we get from the canteen, but we have to pay for ours!'

Martyn sat alone brooding with no knowledge of the time. They had taken his wristwatch from him along with the rest of his property. If prison cells were as depressing and claustrophobic and soul-destroying as this one in which he was now confined he marvelled at how it was the crime rate continued to grow.

It seemed an eternity before he was taken to an interview room, where DI Jackson introduced himself and DS Turpin. When they were all seated at the table, the seal on the interview tape was broken and the tape inserted in the recording machine, and he was cautioned. He didn't take it all in; it sounded just like he had heard on numerous television programmes where scriptwriters had taken pains to get it accurate. It had taken many of them a long time to stop the characters saying...'to be used in evidence *against* you,' it could never be accepted as being *against* them but only in their favour, according the to Judges' rules. Sergeant Turpin had been the one to verify Martyn's particulars and issue the caution. It was the DI who spoke next.

'We are here to investigate the suspicious death of a young woman named Mary Tungate and the disappearance of another named Sally Wainwright. We believe that you can help us in those investigations,' he told Martyn.

Investigations, thought Martyn, shouldn't I be helping with your *enquiries* as the saying goes? Aloud he said, 'Yes I can but I think you should pay a visit to the Plymouth Hoe Guest House where you'll find a woman calling herself Janice Stone, but I believe her name is in fact Sally Wainwright.'

He was about to add that she had told him that she had murdered Mary Tungate, but realised just in time that if he had admitted knowledge of the murder he could be dealt with for conspiracy after the event.

DI Jackson continued, 'The local police have already paid a visit to that address in order to search for and collect any property you may have left there that might help us in the enquiry. The landlady confirms that there was indeed a young woman who arrived with you. Unfortunately for both of us, she left soon after you came in to collect your car. She hasn't returned and we are still looking for her. Can you describe her? You should be able to do that better than Mrs King.'

Martyn gave as full a description as he could, which appeared to satisfy them; no doubt it agreed with that of the person so reported as missing.

'Among the property in your car was a blonde wig,' said Jackson.

'Yes, that's what she was wearing when I first picked her up,' replied Martyn.

'What was your connection with Mary Tungate?'

'I don't know any person called Mary Tungate.'

'At the moment, Mr Burgess, we only have your word for it. You could well have murdered both women and a third may have just escaped your clutches!'

Sergeant Turpin said, 'For the benefit of the tape recording Mr Burgess is shaking his head. Is that a denial?'

'Of course it's a denial. I'm telling the truth, damn it!'

'Do you really think you're going to get away with it? The items we've found in your car are clear evidence that you're involved with three women. One of who has been found drowned in the Thames and the other two are missing.'

Martyn was getting more and more anxious. Surely he couldn't be charged with murder? Two more are missing. What did they mean *two* more. There weren't *two* more!

'I had nothing to do with any Mary Tungate,' he said desperately. 'I didn't know of her, and Sally Wainwright and Janice Stone are the same person, I swear it!' He was exhausted, he was sweating profusely, he was shivering; he was extremely worried.

There was a knock at the door and DC Jones entered and whispered to DI Jackson.

DS Turpin said, 'DC Jones of the Devon and Cornwall Police has just entered the room and after speaking to DI Jackson, DC Jones has now left the room.'

Both officers sat in silence and looked at Martyn making him feel more uncomfortable.

After a while DI Jackson said, 'You may be relieved to know that we do not now suspect you of having anything to do with the disappearance of Sally Wainwright. Her fingerprints lifted from your car and a teacup at the boarding house have been identified as belonging to those of Miss Wainwright, whose prints were found in her flat in London. It is also therefore confirmed that Miss Wainwright and Miss Stone are one and the same.'

Martyn closed his eyes and let out one huge sigh of relief.

'Before you relax too much I must remind you that you are still under caution and the matter of Mary Tungate is still being investigated. It would be in your own interest to make as full a statement as you can. You can't, of course, give evidence of what anyone has told you about which you have no knowledge yourself as that is regarded as hearsay and is not admissible as evidence,' Jackson concluded.

'Of course, I'll tell you all that I know – which in fact is very little,' said Martyn almost in a whisper.

Chapter Eleven

Janice sat on the edge of the bed at the guest house, waiting for the kettle to boil; when it did so it gave a pronounced click and switched itself off. She tore the packets of coffee and sweetener, putting the contents in the cup with the boiled water. For the first time ever, she managed to open the little plastic container of cream without it squirting out all over the place. She sat and stirred her coffee with the plastic spoon provided and watched the bubbles going round and round.

As she gazed at it she half expected to see Mary's face swirling in the eddy. She didn't know what to do. She thought Martyn was a fool to take a chance in collecting the car. But then, why shouldn't he? He had done nothing to be afraid of. But had the police found Mary's purse? Why the hell hadn't she thrown the damn thing away when she had the chance? She would have to run away once again. She only had a few pounds in her pocket.

She drank her coffee while she walked restlessly back and forwards by the window looking out at Mrs King who was hanging out washing from a large basket. Sally supposed running a guest house caused a great deal of washing, with clean bedlinen required for every new visitor. She certainly had a lot of washing there and would be busy for ages.

Well here's my chance, she thought, and she ran downstairs to the deserted kitchen.

At the end of the worktop was a cork noticeboard on which were pinned various notices advertising forthcoming events during the next few months. There were also a number of business cards from local servicemen and repair firms. Mrs King's handbag was laying on the work top next to the board. There was also, under a blue willow-pattern jug, a twenty pound note. She ignored the handbag but quickly snatched the twenty pound note – and then she put it back. Murder and one hundred and seventy-five thousand pounds was one thing but a measly twenty pound note wasn't worth the possibility of the police looking for her for that theft. So she silently left the house.

It was a joy to be out in the fresh air, but after a while she felt the cold begin to penetrate her inadequate clothing. She was getting colder and more miserable every minute. What a hopeless existence her life had been. Why had fate been so cruel to her? She wandered the streets in deep depression.

Chapter Twelve

Reggie Cook, aged nineteen, a trainee chef, rang the bell at 9, Woodlands Terrace, Plymouth. It was a neat red brick terraced house with a small regency bow window in the ground and upper floors both with three panes of bottle glass. The red front door with its highly-polished brass furniture opened directly into the front living room. Mrs Jean White opened the door to the ring.

'Hello, Reginald,' she said, 'go through he's out the back as usual busy with his models.'

She never called him Reggie, just as she always called her son Graham. However, Graham was always inevitably called 'Chalky' by his friends.

As Reggie pushed open the shed door, Chalky hastily shuffled the books he was reading, although it would be more appropriate to say that he was looking at them as opposed to reading them. He pushed them under the plans of the scale model of the *Mayflower*. Chalky was a couple of years older than Reggie, and was in fact the local postman.

'Fuck me, I thought you were my mother. You're a right creep,' he muttered.

'I've left me bovver boots off today in case the Old Bill stopped me going into the match,' replied Reggie.

'Well in future whistle or something when you approach. I got two new mags yesterday,' he said, getting out the 'books' from under the plans of the model that he was working on where he had just hurriedly placed them.

'What d'you think of these?' he asked as he passed them to Chalky.

One was *Dreams – Schwedische Mädchen*, the other *Strip Poker – Ganz in Farben* (in full colour). They were both full of very explicit hard pornography pictures. Both men felt themselves getting hard as they gloated over them.

'Here, help yourself,' said Chalky as he passed a six-pack of Guinness across to Reggie.

'Doesn't your mother wonder why you take so long making your models?' asked Reggie, opening a can.

'No, she thinks her son is a perfectionist,' Chalky replied. He drank a can of stout straight off and then belched ignorantly. 'We'll finish these off and then go.'

Plymouth were at home to Torquay, as near a Local Derby as they would ever get. They arrived earlier than they had intended and killed time in a nearby pub where they consumed more alcohol, much more than was sensible.

'Come on Chalky, it's nearly time for the kick-off. Let's mingle with the Torquay crowd for a bit of fun!' suggested Reggie.

'Not bloody likely! We'd be on our own with no help,' said his friend. Fortunately, even in his inebriated state Chalky was still able to summon some common sense into his increasingly intoxicated thoughts. As it was, they still created havoc, shouting at the ref, the players, the stewards and those around them so much that in order to prevent a more serious breach of the peace the were 'asked' to leave and were escorted from the ground.

'Well, it was a bloody lousy game anyway,' said Chalky with sour grapes as they walked away.

After a while, and a good few streets away from the ground, Chalky nudged Reggie in the ribs.

'Cor look at that!' he said.

They both stared at the knee-length boots, and the very short denim skirt stretched tight across the cheeks of the girl's arse as she strolled aimlessly ahead of them.

'Hello darling!' said Chalky as they caught up with her, 'going our way?'

'Piss off and leave me alone!' came the reply.

'Now that's not very friendly is it? Come on let's go for a little walk,' Reggie said as they took hold of one of Janice's arms each. Walking towards them on the other side of the road were an elderly couple who had a small white poodle trotting along beside them. Janice made a half-hearted struggle in a futile attempt to get out of their clutches, but she didn't cry out for help.

Chalky smiled and waved with his free hand, 'It's all right she's our sister! We're just having a lark.'

The poodle didn't look at all; the poodle's mistress looked straight ahead and pulled her husband hurriedly on with her. He was most willing not to be involved.

The trio turned left into a street lined with plastic cones designating the street as a No Parking area for the influx of vehicles for the football match, and found that it was a cul-de-sac terminating with the open gates to a park. They entered, passing the noticeboard giving the hours that the park was open along with all the bye-laws governing the enclosure. They made their way past the neat flower beds of forget-me-nots, primrose and wallflowers, on past the putting green and through to the far perimeter where they came upon a wooden gate leading through to a walled enclosure designated as a nursery area, where the summer bedding plants were being nurtured under glass cloches.

They ignored the sign proclaiming 'Private – No Public Admittance' and entered. There was no one in attendance, all the gardeners being off duty, and there was no Park Keeper as such, just a fleeting visit by a uniformed man driving a small van with *Park Security Patrol* on the side, who was not due to visit again much before closing time.

Reggie stood behind Janice in the seclusion provided by the high walls of the nursery enclosure, holding both her arms behind her back as he kissed her ears and neck. She could smell the alcohol on his breath. Chalky, standing in front of her, lifted her sweater up under her armpits exposing her amply filled bra, which he pulled up over her breasts. They fell bouncing back into place as they were released from their support. He slid his hand in between her legs and up under her skirt, pushing aside her panties, and forced as many fingers as he could inside her while his other hand squeezed her breasts.

'No, Daddy please, not again Daddy, don't hurt me!' she whimpered.

'What the fuck is she on about?' asked Reggie.

'Who cares, get her on the ground!' said Chalky as he pulled her panties down, eventually getting them over her ankles and boots, and threw them to one side.

Janice stopped whimpering, she didn't scream, she didn't cry any more, she just lay there submissively, with her knees forced up to her shoulders, wide apart as Chalky and then Reggie took her in turn.

Having satiated their lust they ran off leaving her with her skirt rucked up round her waist and her bra and sweater up under her armpits. They didn't stop running for a long time. Unbeknown to one another, they were both filled with remorse for the terrible crime they had just committed upon a poor defenceless human being. They silently vowed to themselves that they would never again degrade themselves by committing such a crime, or any other crime for that matter, ever again.

Janice didn't know how long she had lain there. She wondered why had her father left her there in the cold. The temperature had plummeted, turning the warm spring air into a chill which was getting colder as night began to draw near. She felt her self getting stiff with the cold, which aroused her, and she became aware of a bell clanging and a voice shouting, 'All out, all out! The park is now closing.'

It was some while before Janice came fully to her senses and realised where she was and what had happened. She pulled her bra and jumper down. She noticed her panties laying nearby but she just ignored them and slowly made her way out of the nursery and on out of the park, oblivious of the stare of the man in uniform standing by the partially closed gates. She didn't look at him nor did she speak to him, she just kept on walking, past the noticeboard displaying the bye-laws. Nothing there, she thought, about committing rape on the flower beds.

She kept on walking and wandered the streets in deep depression. As she strolled aimlessly through the shopping precinct she rubbed shoulders with the shoppers, the mothers with their children, the friends and relations, the lovers and sweethearts, all going about their normal apparently happy lives, all unaware of her acute loneliness and desperation. Surrounded by people yet utterly alone, she finally dawdled to a stop and found herself looking in the window of a chemists. She came out after making her purchase. Stupid cow of an assistant, she thought.

'I'm sorry, madam, but we are only allowed to sell one large bottle to any one person at a time,' she had been told.

So what, she thought, there'll be other chemists, and a while later she entered a Boot's where she again purchased one large bottle containing one hundred tablets of Paracetemol to go with the ones she had purchased previously.

Janice felt weary and sought the comfort of the pub that she came upon. She bought and took her drinks from the bar and sat there all alone. It was the warmest she had felt all day; it was the only sensation she could remember feeling all day. Having been walking the streets like a zombie she was glad to rest where she was in the warmth of the pub. She had just consumed her purchases with a glass of lager and was now on her third double whisky which she could feel warming her stomach. She snuggled into the corner of the bench seat on which she was sitting, becoming increasingly drowsy, drifting into a pleasant happy slumber. Soon be passing Brondesbury, she thought. But there would be no jerking train to arouse her this time.

Chapter Thirteen

Detective Constable Bryce Jones and Peter Williams sat in the saloon bar of The Columbus, having a pint of beer each before going home to their respective wives and evening meals to relax in front of the television. They were discussing that day's events. Bryce interrupted Peter's conversation.

'That woman in the corner over there by herself, doesn't she look like the one the Met want to talk to?' he asked.

Peter was already on his feet and they both approached her from opposite sides. She didn't attempt to run as they approached, in fact she ignored them altogether as she sat slumped against the corner of the semicircular bench seat with her eyes closed.

'Excuse me, we'd like a word with you,' said Peter, producing his warrant card for her examination. She didn't look at it.

'Are you all right?' asked Bryce, touching her on the shoulder. She toppled over sideways onto the seat; she was in a deep coma. There was nothing they could do for her; she was still breathing, but only just, so there was no call for resuscitation or heart massage. By the time the ambulance arrived and had conveyed her to hospital she was beyond the help that any stomach pump might have afforded her. She died very soon after arriving.

Martyn had finished making his statement and was waiting to be released on bail pending further enquiries conducive to Sally aka Janice being traced. When DI Jackson came back into the room Martyn assumed he was about to be released and was surprised when he was asked, 'So we are right in believing that you are unaware of the background of Sally Wainwright, known to you as Janice Stone. You've no knowledge of her home, family or friends?'

'No, I haven't. I've put all that in my statement. If I could help you find her I would.'

'No, you don't understand, Mr Burgess. We don't need your help to find her, we have already done so. Unfortunately she has taken an overdose of Paracetemol tablets which has proved to be fatal. We now want to trace some next of kin to inform.'

'Oh my God, the silly little —! I'm sorry, I can't help at all.'

'Well having found her, albeit in such unfortunate circumstances, it lets you off the hook! You are now free to go, our enquiries are now complete as far as we can go,' Jackson told him.

The mortuary attendant prepared the body of Sally Wainwright for the post-mortem and noted that she was not wearing any knickers. In addition to the fact that her stomach contents included alcohol and Paracetemol, it was found that she had very recently had sexual intercourse. In view of this fact, and the absence of any evidence that force had taken place, no importance was placed on the fact that she was not wearing any underpants.

DI Jackson and DS Turpin had returned to London, then to Richmond, Surrey. The crime report had been written up as 'No Crime', there being no evidence to support criminal proceedings. West Hampstead's Missing Person report would now be marked up as 'traced, now deceased'. In the absence of evidence the final inquest on Mary would return an open verdict.

★

Now there was just the two of them looking down into the pauper's grave which the state had provided for Sally in her coffin. The Reverend Hubert Blackstock said a final prayer and Martyn mumbled a faint, 'Amen.' It had the makings of a glorious summery day. The light fluffy white clouds flitting across the bright blue sky like wads of cotton wool did little to prevent the warmth of the sun from beaming down. Even the thrush and blackbirds were obstreperously singing their hearts out. The trees were resplendently dressed all over in green. It was all wrong. No one should be buried on such a lovely day. Such a day should be cold, wet and windy, dull and overcast, with penetrating drizzle. The trees should all be bare standing guard like skeletons. That was the type of weather Martyn had experienced at previous funerals he had attended.

He looked down into the depressing hole that Sally's body would now rest in. How tragic, that a stranger, for that was what he really was, should be the only person in attendance to pay his respects. Routine enquiries had followed their natural course and eventually Mr and Mrs Wainwright were contacted by the police in Coventry.

Neither had shown any remorse or sadness, nor even interest in the news of their daughter's death from an overdose of tablets and no, they didn't want to claim her body. For those in the know this was not surprising. If they weren't interested in their daughter when she was alive they certainly weren't interested in her death. If families couldn't keep together, what chance had nations? There would, always be conflict of some kind somewhere in the world. There would he knew, because of his unanswered prayers of so many years ago, always be people fighting each other. Still, there was one thing you could be sure of, you can't fight with yourself. So he shook hands with the vicar, turned away from the open grave and walked away alone to the car park, with his memories, while the grave digger wasted no time in replacing the earth from where he had recently removed it.

Martyn got into his car, which had now been repaired, and drove away out of Plymouth along Alma Road. Janice's suicide, Martyn couldn't think of her by her true name of Sally, had affected him more than he had at first realised. He looked at the empty seat beside him and felt a spasm of loneliness. Deep in thought he had been driving safely but automatically for quite some time. The day was drawing rapidly to a close, the sun was setting fast in the west.

There ahead at the side of the road stood two figures; two silhouettes standing out in the twilight on the brow of a hill, just like two 'grim reapers'. He gasped as he was suddenly drawn from his reverie. Had they, Janice and the unknown to him Mary, come back to haunt him?

As he passed the two figures, a young man and a young woman they both raised their thumbs in the air, but Martyn kept on going. He looked in his mirror and saw the man give a V-sign. Martyn laughed, And you! he thought, once bitten, twice shy.

Still tucked away, forgotten in Martyn's wallet was Mary's lottery ticket. In five or so months Martyn was to come across it once more and realise that, one hundred and eighty days having passed since it was a winning ticket, it had become null and void and could not be claimed.

Ah well, easy come, easy go, he would think to himself and throw it away, but the memories would always remain with him.